$1.95

LUNCH BOX LIBRARY ™

6 Wild Adventures

BY SARAH ALBEE, RICHIE CHEVAT & KATE MCMULLAN

WORKMAN PUBLISHING · NEW YORK

Lunch Box Library™

6 Wild Adventures

Jacob and the Pirates and *Sarah Zodd's Arabian Nights* copyright © 1997 by Sarah Albee
A Really Bad Cyber-Hair Day and *Creampuff, the Heroic Hamster* copyright © 1997 by Richie Chevat
Revenge of the Mutant Chickens and *The Mummy's Ring* copyright © 1997 by Kate McMullan
Illustrations copyright © 1997 by Eric Brace

Lunch Box Library™ concept by Rosie Behr
Lunch Box Library is a trademark of Workman Publishing Company, Inc., and Rosie Behr

Cover and interior design by Lisa Hollander and Lori S. Malkin
Cover illustration by Eric Brace

Workman books are available at special discounts when purchased in bulk for premiums and
sales promotions as well as for fund-raising or educational use. Special editions or book
excerpts can also be created to specification.
For details, contact the Special Sales Director at the address below.

Workman Publishing Company
708 Broadway, New York, NY 10003-9555

Manufactured in Hong Kong
First printing June 1997

10 9 8 7 6 5 4 3 2

GOOD READING GOES WITH GOOD EATING

LUNCH BOX LIBRARY™ stories are fun for reluctant readers and speed demons alike. Your child can enjoy LUNCH BOX LIBRARY stories even if he or she buys school lunch: Just tuck an episode in a backpack, note-book, or coat pocket. And LUNCH BOX LIBRARY isn't only for lunch. After break-fast, after school with a snack, in the car, or before bed—any time is a good time to read. Here's how it works.

Tear off the title page and "Day One" page from the first story, fold them in half, write a note on the back if you wish, and pack them in your child's lunch bag or box. The next morning, include "Day Two" with lunch, and so on.

There are approxi-mately fifteen episodes in each of the six sto-ries, so each story will last for as many as three weeks of school lunches. Of course, big readers may want to read two or more episodes at a time. Go ahead. It's good for them.

TO ENCOURAGE READING. A book can seem like too big a project for some young readers to tackle. LUNCH BOX LIBRARY is broken into digestible, one-page servings, with an irresistible cliff-hanger concluding each episode.

TO KEEP IN TOUCH DURING A LONG DAY APART. Many parents say they'd like to include a personal note in their child's lunch but are just too rushed in the morning. Each episode provides space on the back for you to write your child a short note.

AS A REWARD FOR GETTING READY FOR SCHOOL ON TIME. Try hiding an episode under a pile of clean laundry as a reward for putting it away. Or ask your child to read a page aloud as you're preparing dinner or before bedtime.

TO SHARE. It's not just for school lunch. Pack an episode in a summer day-camp lunch or mail episodes to your child when you're away on business. Suggest sending episodes to pen pals or grandparents. Children will enjoy sharing these stories with their friends and classmates, with their teachers, and with you.

JACOB AND THE PIRATES

When Jacob Higgins is snatched from his rowboat by a band of pirates, he has no idea what unbelievable adventures await him on the high seas. Will Jacob's quick thinking save him from walking the plank? Will his Hamburger Heaven place mat lead Captain Mulligan Stu to the buried treasure? Find out what pirates really crave in this wild story.

BY SARAH ALBEE

JACOB AND THE PIRATES

My name is Jacob Higgins, but everyone calls me Jake. The story I'm about to tell may sound strange, but believe me, it really happened.

I was visiting my grandparents at their house by the shore. There I was, sitting in my grandfather's little rowboat, fishing. It was one of those hot, mosquitoey summer afternoons, and we had just come back from lunch at Hamburger Heaven. I wasn't really trying to catch any fish. I was just bored, feeling a little sleepy, and eating Chocky Chews. I was trying to get my lower jaw unstuck from my upper jaw when I glanced out to sea. A large, old-fashioned ship had appeared on the horizon. It had black sails. And a black flag.

The ship sailed closer. The flag had a skull and cross-bones on it.

Now, I know practically nothing about ships, but I know a pirate ship when I see one. And this was definitely a pirate ship. A pirate ship? I thought to myself. As in a PIRATE, pirate ship?

I was still wondering how a pirate ship could possibly have sailed up to my grand-parents' seaside house, when suddenly I felt my little boat rock, as though someone had just boarded it behind me. Which is exactly what *had* just happened, since the next thing I felt was a cold steel blade pressing against my neck.

TO BE CONTINUED

LUNCH BOX **DAY** **·1·** LIBRARY

LUNCH NOTES:

JACOB AND THE PIRATES

DAY
·2·

THE STORY SO FAR...

Jacob had just spotted a pirate ship when he felt a cold steel blade pressing against his neck.

"Aye, he's a puny stripling, 'ee is," came a gravelly voice at my ear. I heard another voice grumble in agreement. I glanced at the two men. They looked like pirates. They tied my hands behind my back. I watched my grandparents' house get smaller and smaller as my boat was rowed toward the ship. After a few minutes, we were hoisted up the side, and my boat was tied up. I was thrown roughly onto the deck. I rolled onto my back and found myself staring up at a large, unshaven man with wild black hair, a patch over one eye, and a gold hoop earring in one ear.

"Where be the rest o' the crew?" he bellowed.

"All below decks, Captain," came the shaky reply. "Seasick."

"And they call themselves pirates!" he thundered. "'Tis as calm as a fishpond in June! Snaggletooth Sam! Haul the lily-livered knaves on deck before I carve them into as fine a mince pie as ever a Yorkshire wife cooked of a Sunday!" Snaggletooth hurried below deck. "As for you, young ragged varlet," he said. I guessed he was now talking to me. "Where be the treasure?"

"Treasure?" I echoed, as pleasantly as I could. "I, er, I don't quite know what treasure you mean, sir."

His face clouded. His bushy eyebrows descended into a slant. "He says he knows not where the treasure be!" he boomed to a gray-faced group of pirates that had come tottering toward us. "Have the lying knave walk the plank!"

TO BE CONTINUED

LUNCH BOX **DAY** **·2·** LIBRARY

LUNCH NOTES:

_____

_____

_____

_____

_____

_____

_____

THE STORY SO FAR...

The pirates took Jacob aboard their ship, and the captain ordered him to walk the plank.

JACOB AND THE PIRATES

DAY ·3·

Rough hands

pulled me to my feet. Others hoisted the plank. "Wait!" I cried. "You don't want to get rid of me! I can…cook!" I don't know what made me think of that. I just blurted it out to stall them. I mean, actually, I CAN'T cook much, besides grilled cheese sandwiches.

"Prove it!" said the captain. "Into the galley with ye!" A couple of deckhands picked me up by my elbows and carried me over to a little door. Someone else threw it open, and I was shoved inside. I guessed that galley meant the kitchen, and that I was now in it.

I looked around the tiny, dingy room. There was no cheese in sight. A pot of what I supposed was gruel was bubbling away on the stove. Then I had an idea. "Soup's on!" I called gaily, spooning the vile-looking stuff into unclean wooden bowls. Then I fished out the still half-full box of Chocky Chews from my back pocket. I stirred one Chew into each bowl.

The pirates burst in and grabbed the gruel. They shoveled huge, drippy bites into their mouths.

CHOCKY CHEW

"'Tis wondrous strange," murmured the captain. "Methinks I must get your recipe. In sooth, we have been on the lookout for new recipes, ever since I made the last cook walk the plank. I'll have more." The others held up their empty bowls, too.

"Uh, sorry," I said. "There IS no more."

"THROW HIM TO THE SHARKS!" they cried.

TO BE CONTINUED

LUNCH BOX **DAY · 3 ·** LIBRARY

LUNCH NOTES:

JACOB AND THE PIRATES

DAY .4.

THE STORY SO FAR...

When they heard there was no more food, the pirates decided to throw Jacob to the sharks.

There's nothing like a pack of blood-thirsty pirates, swords drawn, escorting you to the ship's rail, to get your creative gears turning. Luckily, I had another idea.

"HOLD IT!" I yelled. It was loud enough to startle the front of the pack. They stopped in their tracks, which then caused the ones in back to bump into them. This started some cursing and cuffing within the group, and gave me time to search in my pockets. I pulled out the wadded-up placemat from Hamburger Heaven. It had one of those dumb games to color on it, and was covered with French fry grease and ketchup stains. "Here is the treasure map you seek!"

HAMBURGER HEAVEN
MAZE CRAZE

I said, waving the placemat around.

The captain snatched it from my hands. "By my troth, 'ee speaks the truth," he murmured in an awed tone. "As my name be Mulligan Stu, this be the map. Look on it! 'Tis spattered with blood. The boy didst smite down stronger men than 'ee for't, I'll wager."

"Uh, yes," I said gravely, trying to lower my voice. "I didst."

A murmer of admiration rippled through the crowd on deck.

"Lead us to the treasure," commanded Captain Stu.

I just stood there, smiling pleasantly, my brain working furiously on the problem of what to do next. And then we heard the lookout's voice from high above our heads.

"Ship ahoy!"

TO BE CONTINUED

LUNCH NOTES:

_____

_____

_____

_____

_____

_____

_____

JACOB AND THE PIRATES

DAY 5

THE STORY SO FAR...

Jacob promised to lead the pirates to the treasure when the lookout called, "Ship ahoy!"

"Raise the Jolly Roger and prepare for the plunder!" called Captain Stu. I was tied to a mast. The pirates lowered the longboats.

Across the calm water I saw them board the other ship. I could hear shouting and swords clashing. After a while they returned. The sooty, tired pirates dumped a pile of boxes at Captain Stu's feet. He nodded his head, and the boxes were flung open to reveal their contents.

"Fie!" growled Captain Stu. "What is the nature of these orange orbs and strange boots? 'Tis rubbish! Slay the lookout! He saw the ship first!"

"Hold on, hold on," I interrupted. The lookout looked relieved. "This is great stuff you guys plundered! Untie me, please. Thanks. You should be proud of yourselves! New hightops and basketballs! You must have pillaged a sporting-goods shipment!" I opened all the boxes and helped each pirate into a new pair of hightops. I made sure Captain Stu had the nicest pair—purple and black with airpumps and lights. He seemed to like them.

I picked up a ball to show them how to dribble. They seemed pretty impressed. A few had just picked up balls to try for themselves, when we heard the lookout cry out again.

"We are doomed! Look to the port bow! 'Tis the deadly whirlpool!"

TO BE CONTINUED

LUNCH NOTES:

_____

_____

_____

_____

_____

_____

_____

THE STORY SO FAR...

Jacob was just about to teach the crew basketball when the ship drifted into a deadly whirlpool.

The guy steering the ship must have had no time to react. We were sucked straight towards it—a huge, swirling funnel of water right in the middle of the ocean. For a sickening few seconds the ship teetered on the brink of it. Then we were spinning down into the whirlpool. I shut my eyes, but then the next thing I knew, the ship was pitched out again. We seemed to be in a different place. The water looked a little bluer, and the air felt hotter and steamier, as though we were in the tropics.

"Land ho," called the weary lookout. Sure enough, an island had appeared in the distance.

"Let our young prisoner explore the island," called Captain Stu. "If any harm befall him, 'ee won't be missed."

I was in no position to argue. A ladder was lowered and I climbed overboard. We were pretty close to the island, so I was able to paddle to shore using a couple of basketballs to help me float.

I trudged from the water and onto the beach, dripping and tired. Just in front of me was a field of exotic fruits, their leaves rippling softly in the breeze. I headed towards it.

Suddenly I heard a low growl. Turning quickly, I spied a huge beast the size of an elephant, with long hair and dripping fangs and huge claws. It was charging straight at me.

TO BE CONTINUED

LUNCH NOTES:

THE STORY SO FAR...

Alone on an island, Jacob spotted a huge beast charging straight at him.

What would YOU do if a huge, snarling beast lunged for your throat and you happened to be holding a couple of basketballs? Probably the same thing I did, which was to throw a ball at it as hard as I could. But I was still wet from my swim, and my hand slipped as I threw it. The throw went wide. Just when I thought I was history, the beast stopped. It looked at me and then at the ball. Then it turned and chased down the basketball. Clamping it in its enormous jaws, its enormous tail wagging, the creature trotted up and laid the slobbery thing at my feet. Then it sat back, waiting for another throw. A roar of approval went up from the watching

pirates. They splashed ashore, all carrying basketballs. I suggested we pick some fruit to take back with us. I recognized pineapples, melons, and bananas, which were unfamiliar to the pirates. We picked a big pile. Whenever one of the beasts came too close we'd just play fetch with it.

Back on board, I borrowed a dagger from the first mate and cut a chunk from the inside of a pineapple. Luckily I'd watched my mom do it once, so I knew how. Then I offered it to Captain Stu.

"Here, Cap'n," I said. "Try this. It's delicious!"

Captain Stu looked at it, and then his brow darkened. "I see your plan!" he thundered. "Ye think to poison me, ye scurrilous villain! I'll cut ye to shreds!" He drew his sword. So did everyone else.

TO BE CONTINUED

LUNCH BOX **DAY · 7 ·** LIBRARY

LUNCH NOTES:

JACOB AND THE PIRATES

DAY · 8 ·

THE STORY SO FAR...

Captain Stu thought Jacob was trying to poison him with a pineapple.

Swords drawn, the pirates closed in on me. But by now I had begun to read their mood swings. "How about if I try it first?" I suggested cheerfully, and popped the chunk into my mouth. The pirates all took a step back and watched me chew and swallow. "Delicious!" I said.

"I be next, by my troth!" said Captain Stu, and he popped a chunk into his mouth. He swallowed, and then smiled. "'Tis good, forsooth! The boy hast shown us a new recipe!" The rest of the pirates crowded around for a taste. My popularity was growing.

It sure gets boring at sea. With so much time on our hands between plunders, I gave the pirates basketball lessons. We made a hoop from a barrel and some fishing net, and hung it on a mast. It took a while for them to get the hang of it.

"Didst say to shoot?" Cutthroat Clyde asked me once, drawing his revolver and pointing it at a defensive player.

"No, no, the ball! Shoot the ball!" I said hastily. "But not with the gun..."

One day during a heated game, the first mate blocked the bosun's hook shot. I whistled a foul. "Nay!" cried the first mate. "'Twas a clean block!"

"Forswear!" cried the bosun. "'Ee didst strike me upon the arm!" A fight began; threats were made and daggers drawn. Then they decided that it must have been my fault.

"Slay the referee!" cried both teams.

TO BE CONTINUED

LUNCH BOX **DAY · 8 ·** LIBRARY

LUNCH NOTES:

JACOB AND THE PIRATES

THE STORY SO FAR...

The pirate crew preferred to settle a basketball dispute by killing the referee— Jacob, that is.

The lookout

bailed me out again. "Ship ahoy!" he cried. Sure enough, a ship came into view. From the sound of rumba music and clinking glasses, I figured it was a cruise ship. The pirates forgot their argument and bolted in all directions to prepare for the plunder.

I managed to talk Captain Stu into letting me come along. Perhaps I could find some way to escape while the pirates were busy plundering.

"So be it," he agreed. But my heart sank at his next words. "Slay everyone on board!" he cried.

I could see I had to take action before innocent people became fish food. "Uh, Captain?" I said. "May I suggest a different strategy?"

The pirates all stopped what they were doing to hear what I had to say.

"Instead of killing everyone, which would be time-consuming and attract sharks, why not make friends with them? I'll bet their cook would be willing to share some of his recipes with you."

"The boy interests me strangely," mused Captain Stu. "So be it. We'll board the ship and meet the cook! But woe unto him if he doesn't share recipes! We will slay him and everyone else! To the longboats!"

> TO BE CONTINUED

LUNCH BOX DAY ·9· LIBRARY

LUNCH NOTES:

_____

_____

_____

_____

_____

_____

_____

THE STORY SO FAR...

Jacob and the pirates prepared to board a cruise ship and get some new recipes from the cook.

JACOB AND THE PIRATES

DAY · 10

My idea that the pirates join the group had worked. Perhaps too well. Everywhere I looked I saw pirates swimming in the pool, pirates dancing the rumba, pirates playing basketball, pirates exercising. I had to get the pirates off that ship, and keep myself *on* it.

"Hey, great act," a couple with sunblock on their noses said to me as they passed by. "Love the costumes. Where's yours? Aren't you with them?"

"Uh, I-I'm their agent," I said, thinking fast. I couldn't tell them the truth, that they had been invaded by pirates. It might start a panic. I looked around for Captain Stu. I spotted him talking to the cook. They were mixing pink drinks together. "Marry, 'tis better than grog!" Captain Stu was shouting above the noise of the blender.

The cruise director bounded up to me and wrung my hand. "Hey, kid, great act!" he beamed. "The shoes are wrong, but I love the pineapple trick!" I turned in the direction he was looking and was just in time to see Snaggletooth Sam throw a pineapple into the air and hack it into neat, bite-sized chunks with his curved sword, all before it hit the plate. People in Hawaiian shirts applauded.

"Uh, thanks," I said weakly. I had to get them out of here.

And then I heard a voice shriek, "ICEBERG!"

> TO BE CONTINUED

LUNCH NOTES:

JACOB AND THE PIRATES

THE STORY SO FAR...

The pirates were mixing with the passengers— perhaps too well! Then someone yelled, "ICEBERG!"

"Iceberg?" I repeated. "But I could have sworn this was the tropics!" I looked in the direction of the shriek. It was just the first mate, trying ice cream for the first time.

"'Tis wondrous!" he said in the same delighted shriek.

They were never going to leave. I had to think of something.

I grabbed the sleeve of a nearby pirate who was on his way to a step class.

"Scurrilous Ernie!" I said. "Where's Captain Stu?"

"In the galley, learning the onion dip," he said, shaking his arm free and hurrying off.

As I approached the kitchen, I heard the cook explaining a recipe to Captain Stu, who was trying to absorb it.

"My head hummeth like to a hive of bees," he said. "Didst say to add the spice before or after the soured cream?"

"Captain," I said in a low voice. "We're getting near the treasure island."

That got his attention. He was in an uncommonly good mood. "Look!" he said, shoving a card into my hand. It was a bunch of postcards of the cruise ship. Captain Stu had scribbled recipes on the back in crude handwriting. He hurried off to round up the pirates.

Meanwhile, I found a half-empty barrel of something squishy in the kitchen and climbed into it to hide. I heard them clatter away into the longboat, and breathed a sigh of relief. But I breathed too soon. For suddenly, I felt the barrel lurch and rise. The lid was thrown off. I found myself in the longboat, surrounded by angry pirates, their weapons drawn.

> TO BE CONTINUED

LUNCH BOX **DAY · 11 ·** LIBRARY

LUNCH NOTES:

_____

_____

_____

_____

_____

_____

_____

JACOB AND THE PIRATES

DAY · 12

THE STORY SO FAR...

Captain Stu caught Jacob trying to escape, and now he's really angry.

"Ye tarrying, cream-faced loon!" said the first mate. "Trying to escape, were ye? Where be this treasure ye've been promising! Show it forthwith, or we'll hoist you by your feet from the nearest yardarm!"

Just my luck. The cook on the cruise ship had presented the captain with that barrel of sun-dried tomatoes as a going-away present. I've always hated sun-dried tomatoes. We were back on board the pirate ship.

"Fellas, fellas," I soothed, trying to stall for time. "I wasn't trying to stow away. I just, uh, wanted to try these delicious sun-dried tomatoes!" To prove it, I picked one up and tried to chew and swallow it without gagging. "The island is just a few more miles," I coughed, scanning

the horizon wildly for land. "We'll be there before you know it."

This time I don't think they were buying what I was selling. "I'm beginning to think yon bairn knows NOT where the treasure be!" growled Porkrind Pete. "It's Davey Jones' locker for ye, scoundrel." He took a step toward me, his dagger gleaming.

I was in a real jam. I looked for Coast Guard boats. None in sight. And then suddenly the ship lurched. We were all thrown to the deck. We had run aground.

TO BE CONTINUED

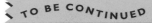

LUNCH NOTES:

JACOB AND THE PIRATES

THE STORY SO FAR...

The pirate ship just ran aground on a rocky island.

"Oops," croaked the exhausted lookout. He followed that up with a sheepish, "Land ho." We'd run the prow of the ship onto a huge outcrop of boulders and were about six feet away from the shoreline.

"Be THIS the treasure island?" the captain asked me in a tone I didn't like very much.

"Yes, this be it," I assured him, hoping I looked sure. We all waded ashore. Several pirates carried shovels and picks on their shoulders. I pretended to consult my bogus map. "This way," I said, pointing to a tic-tac-toe game on my place mat.

"Aye, it says X marks the spot, I'll warrant," said Scurrilous Ernie, looking over my shoulder.

Trudging along, I tried to think of a plan. So far, I'd been able to outwit the pirates. But as soon as they realized there was no treasure, I'd be dead meat. With a heavy heart, I continued trudging.

After an hour or so, they began to grow impatient. "Be we there yet?" demanded Porkrind Pete, who was beginning to huff and puff.

"OK, yeah," I answered wearily. I pointed toward a random palm tree. "Try there," I said. I didn't care anymore. The end was in sight. MY end, that is.

The pirates took turns digging. The minutes ticked by. And then a strange thing happened. We heard a shovel hit something hard. Leaping into the hole, the first mate bent down and picked up something white. "These be bones," he breathed.

TO BE CONTINUED

LUNCH NOTES:

JACOB AND THE PIRATES

THE STORY SO FAR...

While digging for treasure, the pirates uncovered bones under a palm tree.

"Aye," agreed Captain Stu. "Those be the bones of a man, killed by the owner of the treasure so that his soul would guard it forever." The pirates removed their kerchiefs and placed them over their hearts. I didn't say anything, of course, but the bones looked suspiciously like chicken drumsticks to me. Maybe someone had had a picnic there once, I figured. The pirates kept digging.

A shovel clanged again. The diggers scrambled into the hole and dug eagerly with their bare hands. They lifted out a chest. A treasure chest. I know, I know. What are the odds? you're saying. I was amazed, but it was about time something had gone my way.

Captain Stu brushed the dirt off the top of the chest. Everyone, including me, peered down to read the writing on the top:

HERE BE THE TREASURE OF PIEPAN PETE

"Open it!" shouted Captain Stu. Scurrilous Ernie snapped off the rusty lock with the tip of his sword. With a creak, the lid was thrown back. Captain Stu stepped up to the chest and lifted out the only thing inside. It was a book.

"Why, these be the favorite recipes of Piepan Pete himself!" said the Captain reverently. "'Ee was a famous pirate cook, the legend of the seven seas!" He stopped flipping pages for a moment and looked at me. "I had me doubts about 'ee, I'll vouch," he said to me. "But ye've been a stout lad." He clapped me on the back so hard I started coughing. Then he went back to the recipes. While the pirates took turns thumbing delightedly through the book, I crept quietly away.

TO BE CONTINUED

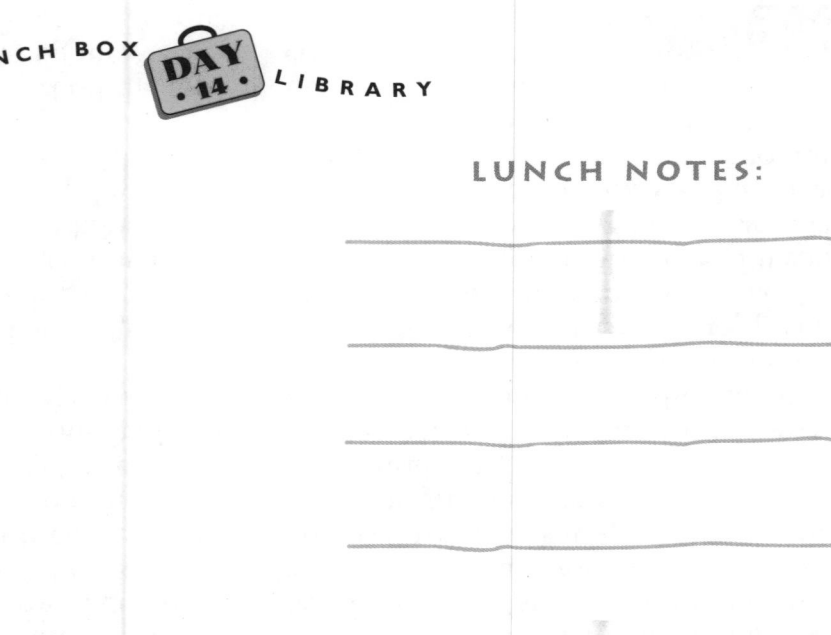

LUNCH BOX **DAY 14** LIBRARY

LUNCH NOTES:

THE STORY SO FAR...

Jacob crept away while the pirates rejoiced over Piepan Pete's recipes.

JACOB AND THE PIRATES

DAY · 15 ·

As soon as I was out of sight of the pirates, I broke into a run for the beach. The island was small; the pirates hadn't realized I'd been leading them in circles to find the treasure. I waded out to the grounded ship and untied my old rowboat. I jumped in and started rowing for the open sea. I was hoping to flag down the cruise ship. It had to be around there somewhere.

Rowing is hard work, in case you've never tried it. I must have rowed for hours. My shoulders ached, my face was sunburnt, and still there was no sign of the cruise ship. It didn't help that the sea was as calm as a fishpond in June. Eventually, I fell asleep.

The next thing I knew, someone was calling my name. It was my grandfather, telling me it was time to come in. I opened my eyes. Sure enough, I was back in my boat in front of their house.

I bet you're thinking that this has turned out to be one of those lame stories where it's all been a dream, right? But don't forget, I promised you that it really happened. Well, I have proof. I found a postcard crumpled up in my pocket. On one side was a picture of a cruise ship. On the other was this recipe:

WITH THE FLAT OF THE SWORD, SMOOTHETH THE BUTTER OF PEANUTS TWIXT TWO SLICES OF BREAD.

ADD JELLY FORTHWITH.

TAKE UP THE EDGE OF THE SWORD AND REND IN TWAIN. SERVE.

Try it sometime. It's delicious.

THE END

LUNCH BOX **DAY · 15 ·** LIBRARY

LUNCH NOTES:

_____

_____

_____

_____

_____

_____

_____

REVENGE OF THE MUTANT CHICKENS

Can a flock of mutant chickens really take over the world? Detectives-in-training Lee Brown and Hugo North discover the ultra-smart chickens' evil plot, but only Lee can save humanity from being turned into people pot pie! Lee's formula for lowering the IQ of a chicken, plus a whole lot of chicken jokes, are all in this April Fools' Day surprise story.

BY KATE McMULLAN

REVENGE OF THE MUTANT CHICKENS

It was a dark and stormy morning. It was eight A.M. on Saturday, April 1, to be exact, when I rang the Norths' doorbell.

Someone answered the door. "Hugo?" I said. "Is that you?"

"It's me," he said, letting me in. "Boy, Lee, you look weird without your glasses."

"*I* look weird?" I squinted at him. "You look like a blur with red fuzz on top." I followed Hugo into the kitchen. "My glasses got stepped on yesterday at soccer practice," I said. "Mom ordered me another pair. They'll be ready on Monday."

I'm Lee Brown. Brown eyes, brown hair. I live next door to Hugo North. We plan to have our own detective agency someday. I'll be the fearless investigator who gets the clues. Brainy Hugo will figure out what the clues add up to. We'll solve the crimes of the century! But

for now, we take whatever comes along.

Which is why I was at Hugo's that morning. Mrs. North had hired us to stay with Hugo's six-year-old sister, Melissa.

"Hi, Lee," Mrs. North said as she walked into the kitchen. She turned to Hugo. "Did you go to the deli?"

"Yes, Mom," Hugo replied. "I got lunch stuff and snacks."

"Don't let Melissa sit in front of her computer all day," she reminded us. "Play Candyland with her. She loves that game. I'll be back from the conference around five." She scribbled some emergency numbers by the phone and took off.

"Check out what I bought at the deli," Hugo said. He threw open the refrigerator door and cried, "Tah-dah!"

LUNCH NOTES:

_____

_____

_____

_____

_____

_____

_____

REVENGE OF THE MUTANT CHICKENS

DAY · 2 ·

THE STORY SO FAR...

Hugo had opened the fridge to show Lee what he'd bought for them to eat.

I squinted into the refrigerator. "What's in it, Hugo?" I had to ask. "I can't see a thing."

"Every kind of junk food ever invented!" Hugo said proudly.

"Wow! It's good your mom didn't look in here!" I said. Mrs. North is a major carrot-stick-and-tofu mom. Hugo is usually a stick-to-the-rules kind of kid. "What possessed you?"

"Who knows?" Hugo shrugged. "But happy April Fools' Day!"

Ten minutes later, Hugo and I were sitting on the couch in the den, watching cartoons. Well, Hugo was *watching* cartoons. Without my glasses, I was more or less listening to them.

Anyway, there we were, munching on Marshmallow Puffs right out of the box, and getting paid three dollars an hour!

"This is the easiest job in the world!" I exclaimed. "At least until we have to play Candyland."

"We won't!" Hugo said. "Melissa's happy up there with her computer. We're happy down here. Why do anything different?"

"You're right," I agreed. "Anyway, how much trouble can she get into, sitting there, staring at the screen?"

"None," Hugo said. "Absolutely none."

"I almost feel bad taking your mom's money," I admitted.

"Not me," Hugo said. "It's not *that* easy."

Lightning flashed, followed by a deafening clap of thunder. And then we heard it — a bloodcurdling scream.

TO BE CONTINUED

LUNCH BOX **DAY · 2 ·** LIBRARY

LUNCH NOTES:

_____

_____

_____

_____

_____

_____

_____

REVENGE OF THE MUTANT CHICKENS

THE STORY SO FAR...

Hugo and Lee were watching cartoons when they heard a bloodcurdling scream.

Hugo and I

jumped up. We bolted up the stairs. We burst into Melissa's room. Melissa was sitting in front of the computer.

"What's wrong?" Hugo cried. "Are you okay?"

"Something scared me," Melissa whimpered.

"What?" asked Hugo. "What scared you?"

"That," Melissa said, pointing to the computer.

I squinted at the screen. All I could see was a fuzzy blur.

"What is it?" I asked Hugo.

"It…it looks like a chicken," he told me. He turned to his sister. "What game is this?" he asked.

"It's not a game," Melissa said. "It's a message."

"From a chicken?" I asked.

"I was playing SimTown," Melissa explained. "All of a sudden there was this awful sound and the computer went off."

"Must have been the lightning," Hugo said. "Go on."

"I waited a few seconds and then I turned the computer back on," Melissa said. "And there was the scary chicken."

"What's so scary about it?" I asked.

Hugo peered at the screen. "It's mean-looking," he said. "It has this big, red comb on its head. And a sharp beak. It's staring. Right at me. The more I look at it …" His voice faded.

"Hugo?" I said. "Melissa?"

But the two of them stood frozen in front of the computer. It was as if that on-line chicken had put them in a trance!

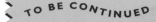

TO BE CONTINUED

LUNCH BOX DAY · 3 · LIBRARY

LUNCH NOTES:

_____

_____

_____

_____

_____

_____

_____

THE STORY SO FAR...

Melissa and Hugo were in a trance, staring at a chicken on the computer.

REVENGE OF THE MUTANT CHICKENS

KA-BOOM!

Lightning flashed and thunder crashed over our heads.

The computer screen went dark.

I glanced at Hugo and Melissa. "Hey, guys?" I said.

They didn't move.

"Guys?" I said, louder this time. I shook Hugo's shoulders. He blinked.

"What...what happened?" he asked.

"You were in a trance or something," I replied. I shook Melissa. In a minute, she snapped out of it, too.

"The chicken told me everything," she said in a flat voice.

"It talked to me, too," Hugo said.

"So, which came first, the chicken or the egg?" I joked.

Hugo didn't laugh. "It told me to relax. Not to worry."

"Let's see if it's still there," said Melissa.

"The chicken?" I said. "But I thought it scared you."

"Let's just see," Melissa insisted, her voice still flat.

"Why do you want to see the chicken?" I asked.

"I just do!" Melissa shrieked. "Turn the computer on!"

I had a feeling that this was no ordinary chicken. And I had a hunch it wasn't working alone.

Melissa was throwing a tantrum now, screaming and kicking. Hugo tried to hold her back from the computer, but she wriggled away from him. She hit ON and the computer powered up.

The screen lit, and there it was—the chicken's partner in crime. "Hugo!" I cried. "It's the Abominable Snowman!"

TO BE CONTINUED

LUNCH BOX DAY 4 LIBRARY

LUNCH NOTES:

_____

_____

_____

_____

_____

_____

_____

THE STORY SO FAR...

Lee saw the Abominable Snowman on the computer.

REVENGE OF THE MUTANT CHICKENS

DAY · 5 ·

"Lee," Hugo said, "you should get a spare pair of glasses." I squinted at the screen. "It's not the Snowman?"

"It's the chicken," Hugo said. "And I was wrong. It doesn't really look mean. Or scary. It looks... sort of friendly."

"Careful, Hugo," I warned him. "We have to figure out what's with this chicken. So don't go getting hypnotized again, okay? Okay, Hugo?"

Hugo didn't answer. He and Melissa stared at the screen.

"Not again!" I groaned. I turned the computer off.

Hugo and Melissa didn't move. I waved my hand in front of Hugo's eyes. He didn't blink. "Hugo?" I said, "Hugo! Snap out of it!" I shook him harder this time. But his blue eyes only stared into space. I stepped up and yelled in his ear: "Hugo!"

Finally Hugo's eyes fluttered.

When he saw me, he said, "Oh, Lee. Hi."

"Boy, that's one powerful chicken," I said.

As soon as he heard the word "chicken," Hugo changed. "The chicken," he said, his voice flat, the way Melissa's had been. He stared straight ahead and said, "I want to see the chicken."

What was it with this chicken, anyway? It had turned my best friend and his sister into zombies! I had to take action! Drastic, extreme action!

It wouldn't be easy, but I knew what I had to do.

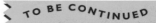

TO BE CONTINUED

LUNCH NOTES:

REVENGE OF THE MUTANT CHICKENS

DAY 6

THE STORY SO FAR...

Lee was about to take action to bring Hugo and Melissa out of another trance.

I ran down to the kitchen. I opened the freezer and slid out an ice cube tray. Then I ran back upstairs and started dropping ice cubes down Hugo's neck. At first he only muttered. Then he started shivering. At last he jumped up and yelled, "Stop it!"

"That's better," I told him. "Now the same for your sister."

It took six cubes down the back of her sweatshirt before Melissa started shrieking, "Lee! Cut it out!"

"Sorry," I told both of them. "But I had no choice."

I herded Hugo and Melissa down to the kitchen. I ran into the den and flipped on the TV for a second. The chicken was on every channel! I turned it off and ran back to the kitchen.

"So," I began, "tell me what the"—I knew better than to say the word *chicken* again—"what you heard."

Hugo frowned. "Over and over, a voice kept telling me not to worry," he said. "That I'd be in such a nice warm place."

"That's what it told me, too," Melissa said.

"But what are you not supposed to worry about?" I asked.

"The chickens," Melissa said simply. "They're taking over Earth."

I stared at Melissa. Had staring at that chicken's face turned her brain into scrambled eggs? Or was our planet really in danger of being overrun by a band of evil, mind-bending poultry?

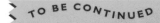

TO BE CONTINUED

LUNCH BOX **DAY · 6 ·** LIBRARY

LUNCH NOTES:

THE STORY SO FAR...

Melissa just announced that the chickens planned to take over Earth.

REVENGE OF THE MUTANT CHICKENS

DAY · 1 ·

"No way," I said. "Chickens are too dumb to take over!"

"These chickens have mutated," Hugo said. "You know, changed. They're intelligent, Lee. Really intelligent. They've already taken over our nation's computer system."

"You mean that virtual chicken is appearing on computer screens all over the country?" I asked.

Hugo nodded.

"This is horrible!" I cried. "We have to stop them!"

"How? We don't know where the real chickens are," Hugo said.

"I do," Melissa said. "Chicken Command Headquarters is in the Plastico Chemical Building downtown."

"That's only a few blocks from here," I exclaimed. I pictured the tall skyscraper with the dark mirrored windows. "We could ride our bikes over there right now!"

"Are you nuts?" Hugo asked. "That chicken almost took over our minds on computer! Think what it would do to us in person!"

"You're right," I said. "It's too risky. I'll call the police!" I dialed the number Mrs. North had written by POLICE.

A man picked up. "Eighth precinct. Officer Rogers speaking."

"Officer! This is Lee Brown. I'd like to report a takeover of the United States computer system by... by... enemies!"

"Don't worry," Officer Rogers told me. "Go turn on your computer again. You'll be in a nice warm place. You'll see."

I slammed down the phone. "The chickens!" I cried. "They've taken over the police!"

TO BE CONTINUED

LUNCH BOX DAY 7 LIBRARY

LUNCH NOTES:

_____

_____

_____

_____

_____

_____

_____

REVENGE OF THE MUTANT CHICKENS

"Everyone who's used a computer or looked at TV today is mind-controlled by chickens!" I yelled. "We have to stop them!"

"What are we waiting for?" asked Melissa. "Let's go!"

We ran outside. The rain had stopped. We got our bikes and took off.

I managed to keep the blur I knew as Hugo in sight as I rode. We made it to the Plastico Building in ten minutes. We shoved our bikes into the bike rack, ran up the sidewalk and into the lobby. Someone was at the guard's station. I squinted. It looked to me like a bride, but it was . . .

"A chicken the size of a polar bear!" Hugo cried.

The guard chicken strutted over to us. "All right," she said in a deep voice. "What are you doing here?"

"We want to see the chicken in charge," Hugo managed.

The guard chicken opened a cell phone and punched in a few numbers with her wing tip. She clucked softly into the phone, fixing us with a beady eye. Then she snapped the phone shut.

"The Commander-in-Chicken cannot be disturbed," she said.

Melissa grabbed Hugo's arm and yanked him across the lobby and into an elevator. I ran after them.

"Hey!" the chicken guard called. "You can't go up there!" Her final words rang out as the elevator doors closed: "You'll be sorry!"

TO BE CONTINUED

LUNCH BOX **DAY · 8 ·** LIBRARY

LUNCH NOTES:

THE STORY SO FAR...

Lee, Hugo and Melissa just ran into an elevator at Chicken Command Headquarters.

REVENGE OF THE MUTANT CHICKENS

DAY ·9·

"Press PENTHOUSE," Melissa told Hugo.

The Plastico Building had 48 floors, and we were headed for the top. At last the elevator slowed down and stopped. The doors opened. Waiting to greet us in the hallway stood a pair of giant chickens.

"Step out of the elevator and no one gets hurt," ordered the biggest one. We did.

They walked us to a small room furnished with only a few plastic chairs. A huge computer screen took up one whole wall.

"We'll be back," the big chicken said, slamming the door.

I took a fast look at the screen. I caught a glimpse of a big, blurry form that I guessed was the hypnotizing chicken.

"Don't look at it, Lee," Hugo said. "You either, Melissa."

Melissa didn't answer.

I squinted over at her. She was gazing up at the screen.

"Melissa!" I cried. "Cut it out! Look down at the floor!"

But she kept staring.

"Hugo!" I cried. "Do something! Cover up your sister's eyes! Don't let her stare at the chicken!"

"It's too late, guys," Melissa said.

"Too late?" I cried. "Too late for what?"

"Too late," she said again. "But don't worry! We're going to be so nice and warm. Everything's going to be all right."

TO BE CONTINUED

LUNCH NOTES:

_____

_____

_____

_____

_____

_____

_____

THE STORY SO FAR...

The three have been taken prisoner at Chicken Command Headquarters.

REVENGE OF THE MUTANT CHICKENS

DAY 10

I gasped. "The chickens have taken over Melissa's mind!"

"Oh, no!" Hugo moaned. "Mom's going to kill me!"

"It's not bad," Melissa volunteered. "It happened the third time the chicken hypnotized me. I mean, didn't you guys wonder how I knew where Chicken Command Headquarters was?" She walked over and knocked three times on the door. A chicken opened it. Melissa spoke softly to her with a series of *clucks* and *blucks*.

"Good grief!" Hugo whispered. "She speaks poultry!"

Now Melissa turned toward us. "Come on," she said. "The Commander-in-Chicken will see us now."

"We should have played Candyland with her," Hugo fretted as we followed Melissa and the giant chickens down the hall.

"Hugo," I whispered, "what do you think the chicken means when it says *don't worry* and *you'll be nice and warm?*"

"Maybe they're flying us to Florida?" he suggested.

I gave Hugo a look. Was he kidding? I didn't think so. He'd been hypnotized twice by the chicken. Melissa's mind had gone over to the chickens after three times. Suddenly I understood. Hugo had only a third of his usual brain power left! He was still smarter than most people, but one more eye-lock with the cyber-chicken, and he'd be a goner.

We walked until we came to a huge wooden door. If the real hypno-chicken was behind it, it was bye-bye Hugo. And mine might be the only fully functioning human brain left on the planet!

Normally, I am a fearless person. But *that* was scary!

TO BE CONTINUED

LUNCH BOX **DAY 10** LIBRARY

LUNCH NOTES:

THE STORY
SO FAR...

Hugo and Lee
were following
Melissa to see
the Commander-
in-Chicken.

REVENGE OF THE MUTANT CHICKENS

An enormous chicken sat behind a desk. She had "commander" written all over her. Other chickens sat hunched over computers.

"These kids are resisting, Commander," the guard said.

Melissa spoke up. "Oh, most royal Commander-in-Chicken?"

The Commander glanced up. "Yes? What is it?"

"My brother, Hugo, has had two chicken trances," she said. "One more, and he'll be with us. But Lee can't see the computer screen," she went on, explaining about my glasses. "So I thought maybe it would work if you explained things."

The Commander-in-Chicken glanced at the wall clock. "I'll give you the quick story," she said. "I was hatched on the Foster Farm across the river from the Plastico Chemical Plant. One night, Plastico dumped chemical sludge into the river. The next day, we chickens drank the river water; our IQs zoomed up 150 points and we quadrupled in size.

"By nightfall we had escaped our coops and left the Foster Farm," the Commander-in-Chicken went on. "We pecked through a window in the Plastico plant, and holed up in the basement. At night, we had the plant to ourselves. In no time, we learned English and mastered the computer systems." The Commander shrugged. "The rest, as they say, is history. By this time tomorrow, *chickens* will be the dominant life-form on the planet!"

The Commander fixed me with her beady eye. "Now," she said, "I have a question for *you*. Why did the chicken cross the road?"

TO BE CONTINUED

LUNCH BOX **DAY · 11 ·** LIBRARY

LUNCH NOTES:

_____

_____

_____

_____

_____

_____

_____

THE STORY SO FAR...

The Commander-in-Chicken just asked Lee why the chicken crossed the road.

REVENGE OF THE MUTANT CHICKENS

"Uh...to get to the other side," I answered.

"People think that's funny," the Commander-in-Chicken said. "But it *isn't* funny! And neither is this one: What's Snow White's brother's name? Egg White! Get the yolk?"

"Oh, that's bad," I said, wanting to stay on her good side.

One of the other chickens glanced up from her computer. "How about this? Why did the chicken go halfway across the road?"

"Got me," I said.

"To lay it on the line!" the chicken answered.

Another chicken called, "Why did the hen stop laying eggs?"

"I don't know," I said.

"She was tired of working for chicken feed!" she said.

"Here's one!" called another chicken. "Why did the chicken get kicked out of school? For using fowl language!"

"Boy," I said. "You chickens sure know a lot of jokes."

"You probably think we only know *corny* ones," growled the Commander-in-Chicken.

"Not at all," I assured her quickly.

The Commander nodded. "All right, girls. Back to work," she said. "We have to get on with our plan."

"Excuse me, Your Highest Empress Chicken?" I said meekly. "When you take over the earth, what happens to people?"

"Ever hear of *revenge,* Lee?" the Commander-in-Chicken asked, her beak curving up in a cruel smile. "How about people pot pie!"

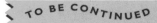

LUNCH BOX **DAY 12** LIBRARY

LUNCH NOTES:

THE STORY
SO FAR...

The Commander-
in-Chicken just
told Lee that
the chickens
want revenge.

REVENGE OF THE MUTANT CHICKENS

"You're going to *eat* us?" I cried. "When the cyber-chicken talked about a nice, warm place, she meant the *oven?*"

"What's the problem? You've been eating us for centuries!" the Commander said. "Now it's our turn. Mmmm, I can't wait to get my beak around an order of French fried fingers!"

I squinted over at Melissa. She was still smiling. These feathered fiends had brainwashed her completely!

The Commander turned to the guard. "Take them back to the computer room," she ordered.

My mind was whirling. I had to think of a way to stop these crazed chickens, or I'd end up under a flaky pie crust!

"How many of you super chickens are there?" I asked.

"Only a dozen," she admitted. "But once we take over, we plan to lay plenty of eggs."

"Since you left the farm," I went on, "you've only been in a chemical plant and in this steel-and-glass office building?"

"So?" The Commander-in-Chicken frowned. "What's your point?"

"Before you take over," I said, "wouldn't you like to spend some time inside a real, human home? There are nice, soft chairs. TV with hundreds of channels. Big refrigerators full of snacks. Plus you could see how humans live. That might come in handy."

The Commander turned and huddled with the other chickens.

"Don't worry!" I whispered to Hugo. "I have a plan!"

Then she said, "We shall come to your home now."

Hugo whispered, "My mom's going to kill you, Lee!"

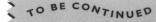
TO BE CONTINUED

LUNCH BOX **DAY 13** LIBRARY

LUNCH NOTES:

REVENGE OF THE MUTANT CHICKENS DAY·14

THE STORY SO FAR...

Lee invited the chickens over to Melissa and Hugo's house.

We led the way to Hugo's. The chickens flocked into the house, clucking over the tasteful furnishings.

"Come into the den!" I called. "Here, Commander-in-Chicken, you take the recliner. The rest of you, put your feet up. Make yourselves comfortable! You, too, Melissa. I'll just turn on the TV. . ." I grabbed the remote and did a bit of surfing. "Oh, perfect!" I said. "A rerun of *Gilligan's Island.* You'll love it!"

When the chickens were settled, I hurried into the kitchen. I piled high a tray with Ice Cream Nuggets, Chocolate Swirl Pudding, cans of soda. I got out potato chips, cheese whirls, taco-flavored corn chips, candy bars, and cereal—Marshmallow Puffs, Choco-Bits, and Sparkle Flakes. I carried it all into the den.

"Here you go," I said, passing the tray around. "Take more chips. Here, let me help you unwrap that cupcake!"

I kept the goodies coming. When *Gilligan's Island* was over, I found *The Brady Bunch,* followed by *Bewitched* and *I Dream of Jeannie.* The chickens sat there, clucking and burping contentedly. But they weren't, I noticed, speaking much English any more. I kept delivering snacks and finding just the right TV shows. I didn't let up for a second.

"What a mess!" Hugo said at last. "Crumbs all over the floor."

Melissa peered out the window. "Hey, Hugo!" she called. "Mom's home!"

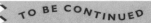

TO BE CONTINUED

LUNCH BOX DAY · 14 · LIBRARY

LUNCH NOTES:

THE STORY SO FAR...

The chickens were making a huge mess in the den when Mrs. North arrived.

"Keep her out of the den, Hugo!" I yelled. "Melissa, stay with the chickens! Make sure they're still watching *Mr. Ed.*"

Hugo and I ran to the kitchen. Mrs. North walked in from the garage. She looked tired. "Hi," she said. "Where's Melissa?"

"She's taking a little rest," Hugo said.

Mrs. North nodded. "I feel dizzy, like I'm coming down with something. I think I'll put my feet up, and watch the news."

"Uh, the TV in the den broke," Hugo said.

Mrs. North groaned. "Well, I'd better take a look at it."

"You can't!" Hugo exclaimed. "I called the TV repair shop and they sent someone over to pick it up. So it's gone."

Mrs. North looked sicker than ever. "Well, maybe I'll just go put my feet up and read the paper."

"But not in the den!" Hugo said. "See, the TV repair man wasn't feeling too good, and while he was here, he got sick."

"Sick?" Mrs. North exclaimed. "With what?"

"Uh...chicken pox." Hugo's brain was definitely not in top form. "We shouldn't go into the den or we might catch it."

Mrs. North closed her eyes. "Maybe that's what I'm getting," she muttered. "Chicken pox. Maybe I'll go have a bath."

Hugo let out a huge sigh of relief as his mother walked up the stairs to her room.

"Come on," I told him. "We have to check the chickens."

We raced to the den. When Hugo saw what had happened in there, he gasped. But I smiled. My plan had worked like a charm.

TO BE CONTINUED

LUNCH NOTES:

_____

_____

_____

_____

_____

_____

_____

REVENGE OF THE MUTANT CHICKENS DAY ·16·

A dozen small chickens roosted in the den. Their brains combined couldn't take over a coop, much less the planet.

"I figured if chemicals turned regular chickens into super chickens," I explained, "then the process might work in reverse."

"But what chemicals did you give them?" Hugo asked.

"Trisodium phosphate, pyridoxine, hydrochloride…"

"Ah!" Hugo nodded. "The junk food!"

"The old reruns simply speeded up the process," I added.

We herded the chickens into cardboard boxes and called Foster Farm. Ten minutes later, Mr. Foster drove up in his truck. He was so happy to have his missing chickens back that he didn't even ask how they'd ended up at Hugo's.

After that, Hugo and I ran back into the den to straighten up. That's when we found Melissa, sound asleep on the couch.

Hugo poked her. "Wake up, Melissa. Help us clean up."

Melissa yawned and said, "I had the weirdest dream!"

"Do you think we should relax, Melissa?" I asked her.

"You think everything's going to be all right?" Hugo added.

Melissa frowned. "What are you talking about?" she asked.

Hugo grinned at me and we started dust-busting the den. We finished just as Mrs. North walked in.

"Hugo!" she exclaimed. "The TV's right there! Why did you tell me that silly story?"

What Hugo did then let me know his genius brain was back in working order. He smiled and said, "April Fool, Mom!"

THE END

LUNCH BOX **DAY · 16 ·** LIBRARY

LUNCH NOTES:

A REALLY BAD CYBER-HAIR DAY

Can a girl in the 23rd century defend Earth against an alien invasion and get her hair done at the same time? Twelve-year-old Kyla Ion was only trying to look nice, but when the Weezliks decided to invade her apartment, something had to be done. With a little help from her human and robot friends, Kyla triumphs in this fast and funny story from the future.

BY RICHIE CHEVAT

A REALLY BAD CYBER-HAIR DAY

"Oooh! Mega Gross!"

Twelve-year-old Kyla Ion looked at the 3-D image of herself in the holo-mirror and made a face. The floating hologram made a face right back at her.

"I thought this was the 23rd century!" she cried. "How come we can put a woman on Pluto but can't get rid of bad hair days?"

Kyla tugged at the thick mop of hair. It just wasn't right. Oh, the colors were the ones she wanted—green, orange, pink and purple. And the style was right—the strands were twisted together in tight braids. But it just wasn't *moving*. Cyber hair was supposed to dance around. Kyla's just lay there like a bowl of limp syntha-spaghetti.

"This darned cyber hair," Kyla groaned. "It's impossible to program! If only Mom and Dad would let me get a Style-O-Matic Beautifier Computer of my own."

A sly grin came over Kyla's face, and an instant later she was in her parents' room in front of the Style-O-Matic. She fished the cyber-hair cable link from behind her ear and plugged her head into the computer. Immediately, a peppy voice said, "Hair program. Let's make you look maaarvelous!"

"You bet!" Kyla answered and pressed a button on the computer.

Suddenly the lights in the whole apartment began to flash and an ear-splitting buzzer shook the air.

"Warning!" a metallic voice barked. "Weezlik attack! Weezlik attack! Prepare for battle!"

Kyla stood rooted to the spot. The Weezliks! The dreaded alien invaders who had almost destroyed Earth! They were back and they were coming to invade her apartment!

TO BE CONTINUED

LUNCH NOTES:

_____

_____

_____

_____

_____

_____

_____

A REALLY BAD CYBER-HAIR DAY

THE STORY SO FAR...

Kyla Ion was programming her cyber hair when the Weezlik alarm sounded.

"Weezliks!" Kyla shouted. "Help!"

"You *will* need help if your parents catch you using their Style-O-Matic," said a voice.

The alarm buzzer stopped as suddenly as it had started. Ethel 417B, Kyla's robo-tutor, hovered her way into the room.

"Ethel!" Kyla shouted angrily. "That was a dirty trick!"

The robot wagged a silver-colored finger at the girl.

"Your data banks are obsolete," she lectured. "The Weezliks were defeated ten years ago."

"Everybody knows that," Kyla shot back. "But they might come back. That's why every house has Weezlik detectors."

"Correct. But my programming still shows you should spend less time fixing your hair and more time upgrading your brain," the robot answered.

"Come on, Ethel," Kyla complained. "I aced my last hypno-tests."

"True," Ethel nodded her metallic head. "But there's always room for improvement."

"Just let me finish programming my hair," pleaded the girl, and without waiting for an answer, she hit some buttons on the computer.

"You're doing it wrong!" Ethel warned. Kyla looked at the screen, which was flashing bright orange, and made a frantic grab to detach her cyber-hair cable. It was too late.

"Warning! Warning!" cried the computer's voice. "Galactic Net Error!"

"What's that mean?" Kyla asked nervously.

"Incomplete data," Ethel replied slowly. "But my calculations indicate you really messed up—big time!

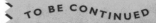
TO BE CONTINUED

LUNCH BOX · DAY · 2 · LIBRARY

LUNCH NOTES:

_____

_____

_____

_____

_____

_____

_____

THE STORY SO FAR...

Kyla's accidentally set off a Galactic Net Error with her Style-O-Matic hair computer.

A REALLY BAD CYBER-HAIR DAY

ZEEE! CRASH!

A deafening racket, like a magneto-blaster zapping a low-flying gravity sled, filled the apartment.

"It's coming from the kitchen," Ethel said calmly, as she headed for the door. "Come on!"

"You mean, *walk?*" Kyla asked in disbelief. "What do you think they invented teleporters for?"

"Try it!" Ethel commanded. "It's just down the hall."

With a sigh and a shrug, Kyla followed her robot tutor down the long hallway and into the kitchen. It was total chaos. The Chef-O-Rama food replicator was spitting out plates of Martian meat loaf. The Cryo-fridge was trying to freeze the compu-dog, which was howling and chewing on the D.D.D. (Dirty-Dish Destructor). The micro-maid had gone

nuts and was mopping the floor with about ten gallons of meteor pudding!

"What's going on?" Kyla yelled over the racket of meteors hitting the floor.

"Somehow your hair program interfaced with the kitchen computer," Ethel 417B answered as she plugged a silvery finger into a control panel socket. "I believe it's possible to…" The automated machines froze in their tracks. But a metallic voice began shouting.

"Warning! Weezlik attack! Weezlik attack! Prepare for battle!"

"Come on, Ethel," Kyla groaned. "How many times are you going to pull that corny joke?"

Ethel's silvery face frowned. "I did not activate the alarm. In fact, I can verify that there really are…"

TO BE CONTINUED

LUNCH NOTES:

_____

_____

_____

_____

_____

_____

_____

THE STORY SO FAR...

Ethel's not joking. There really are Weezliks attacking Kyla's apartment.

A REALLY BAD CYBER-HAIR DAY

DAY 4

"Weezliks!"

Kyla screamed as the entire wall of the apartment disappeared in a flash of bright light. Kyla could see a Weezlik landing craft hovering in the air next to her building. A moment later a hatch in the space ship opened and a real, live Weezlik stepped into Kyla's kitchen. Its bright purple tongue flashed in and out. Its yellow eyes gleamed. It stuck out one of its 15 long, razor-sharp claws and scratched the floor.

"Hmm," it croaked. "Meteor pudding. Real meteors, too!"

"What do you want, Weezlik?" Kyla demanded angrily.

"That's Weezlik Commander Gerkin to you, earthling," the alien sneered. "And what we want is simple—your hair!"

"Oh, do you like it?" Kyla said, feeling pleased in spite of herself. "I've been working on it all morning."

"We don't care about your hair *style!*" the alien hissed. "It's the programming. You have the plans for our next invasion of Earth!"

"The Galactic Net Error," whispered Ethel. "Somehow their plans are in your cyber hair."

"Correct, robot creature," Commander Gerkin said. "And we must have them back. The Weezlik task force is already in orbit!"

"But I thought you guys were defeated ten years ago," Kyla said.

"A nasty rumor," the Weezlik replied angrily, "We only went on vacation. Now give us your hair!"

"No way!" Kyla shouted defiantly. "Over my dead body!"

"With pleasure," Gerkin said calmly. The next thing Kyla knew she was looking right down the barrel of a sonic disruptor!

TO BE CONTINUED

LUNCH NOTES:

A REALLY BAD CYBER-HAIR DAY

DAY · 5 ·

"Surrender your hair," the Weezlik commander repeated.

"Sorry, Bub," Kyla replied. "But I'm kind of attached to it. Besides, I like Earth the way it is—and I don't like Weezliks!"

Two more Weezlik warriors ran out of the space ship and into the kitchen.

"Take her aboard," Commander Gerkin ordered. "And blast the robot."

"What do we do now?" Kyla asked Ethel.

"I'm programmed for instruction, not armed self-defense," Ethel explained. "Would you like me to prepare a study guide on fighting Weezliks?"

"Study!" Kyla moaned. "I wish I *had* studied instead of spending so much time watching music holograms on MHV." The two Weezlik soldiers moved toward them. Kyla's mind searched for a way out.

"Music holograms!" she thought. "That gives me an idea!"

She reached out to the control panel and punched a button. Instantly two six-foot spiders and a seven-foot-tall kangaroo appeared in the middle of the kitchen.

"Oooh, baby!" the kangaroo screamed. "You're so cosmic! It's astronomic!" The spiders answered, "Whoo whoo!" and rocked wildly back and forth.

"Commander!" shouted one of the soldiers, its alien voice cracking with what sounded like fear. "What is it?"

"I don't know!" the commander shouted back. "Shoot it!"

Kyla heard the whine of the Weezlik disrupters being turned on.

"Run!" Kyla shouted to Ethel as the blasts shook the room. "Run!"

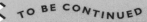

TO BE CONTINUED

LUNCH BOX **DAY** LIBRARY
· 5 ·

LUNCH NOTES:

THE STORY SO FAR...

The Weezliks fired their sonic disrupters at Kyla and Ethel.

A REALLY BAD CYBER-HAIR DAY

DAY · 6 ·

KABOOM!

The sonic blasts ripped away part of the door frame as Kyla and Ethel darted through. But the Weezliks were too scared of the giant spiders and kangaroo creature to follow.

"What was that?" Ethel squawked as they fled down the hall.

"Eddie and the Arachnoids!" Kyla shouted back. "It's their latest music holo-video. Aren't they, like, total space fave?"

"Well, they *did* scare the Weezliks," Ethel admitted.

"Not for long, though," said Kyla. She pulled Ethel onto a teleporter disk and pressed a button. Nothing happened.

"The Weezliks must have jammed the circuits," said Ethel. "Let's use the anti-gravity boards!"

Kyla was shocked. "Go *outside*? I was outside last week!"

"Come on!" yelled Ethel. A few seconds later, she and Kyla were in the sky garage, climbing on a long, flat anti-gravity board. Kyla started it and they flew out into the sky two miles above the city.

"They're right behind us!" yelled Ethel.

Looking over her shoulder, Kyla saw the Weezliks back at the apartment tower, climbing on their own anti-gravity boards.

"Don't worry," Kyla boasted. "Just watch me cloud surf."

At that instant the giant head and shoulders of a fierce-looking man appeared in the air in front of them. A hand the size of a small building reached down right into their path.

The giant thundered in an angry, commanding voice:

"STOP!"

TO BE CONTINUED

DAY
· 6 ·

LUNCH NOTES:

_____

_____

_____

_____

_____

_____

_____

A REALLY BAD CYBER-HAIR DAY

THE STORY SO FAR...

Kyla and Ethel escaped by hopping an anti-gravity board, but a giant commanded them to stop.

Kyla looked up at the huge face that floated in their path.

"Officer," she said with relief. "Am I glad to see you!"

"Young lady," the holographic image boomed. "Do you know you're speeding? Slow down! By order of the Parking Meter and Hovering Vehicles Bureau!"

"But, officer," Kyla protested. "I'm being chased by Weezliks!"

"Don't give me that one," the holographic image sneered. "Everyone knows the Weezliks were defeated ten years ago!"

"But, but..." Kyla sputtered.

"Now, Kyla," Ethel lectured. "Remember, the Parking Meter and Hovering Vehicle Police are your friends."

"Ethel!" Kyla snapped. "Whose side are you on?"

"Sorry about that," Ethel apologized.

"It's in my programming."

"Forget about it!" Kyla shouted at the hologram. "I'm not slowing down for anyone!" She kicked the speed control and the board zoomed ahead.

Then, without warning, the board under her feet began to slow down. Frantically, Kyla jabbed at the toe controls with her foot. The board kept slowing and now the Weezliks were gaining fast!

"Ethel!" Kyla shouted. "What's happening to the board?"

"Perhaps the Weezliks are using some sort of tractor beam," Ethel shouted.

"Attention," boomed the now-familiar voice. "Your vehicle is now under the control of the P.M.H.V.P. A safe speed limit *will* be maintained."

"Safe?" Kyla screamed. "It won't be safe if those Weezliks catch up!"

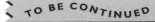

TO BE CONTINUED

LUNCH NOTES:

_____

_____

_____

_____

_____

_____

_____

THE STORY SO FAR...

The Police took control of Kyla's anti-gravity board, and the Weezliks are catching up.

A REALLY BAD CYBER-HAIR DAY

DAY · 8 ·

"They're getting closer!" Ethel reported. "Capture is highly probable!"

"Not yet!" Kyla replied. Quickly, she raised her wrist hyperlink to her mouth. "Connect to Pizza Web!" she commanded.

"Kyla," Ethel gasped. "This is no time to think about eating!"

A hologram of a pizza chef appeared next to the speeding board.

"Two dozen Galactic Specials, please," Kyla ordered. "They're for the board just behind me. And make it snappy!"

The hologram nodded and vanished.

"Kyla, I don't see how pizzas…" Ethel began.

"Just watch," Kyla interrupted.

As she and Ethel watched, a flying pizza delivery robot rocketed up from the ground right into the path of the oncoming Weezliks! The Weezliks' boards were forced to stop.

"I've got to see this," Kyla laughed as they zoomed away. She pressed a button on her hyperlink and an image of the Weezlik commander appeared in the air next to them.

"We don't eat pizza—we're Weezliks!" he was shouting at the robot delivery craft.

"Don't give me that one," sneered the robot. "Everyone knows the Weezliks were defeated ten years ago. Now pay up!"

"That'll keep them busy while we hide somewhere," Kyla said as she switched off the remote image. "And I know just the place!"

She steered the board down through some clouds, toward a huge glass and steel dome that floated above the ground.

Ethel 417B saw where they were going. "No, Kyla," she pleaded. "Not there! Anyplace but there!"

TO BE CONTINUED

LUNCH BOX DAY ·8· LIBRARY

LUNCH NOTES:

_____

_____

_____

_____

_____

_____

_____

A REALLY BAD CYBER-HAIR DAY

THE STORY SO FAR...

Kyla sent the Weezliks a phony pizza order; now she's heading for the perfect hiding place.

"I can't believe it!" Ethel declared as the board set down in a parking lot. "We're being chased by Weezliks and you want to go to the *mall!*"

"They'll never think of looking for us here," Kyla said as she hurried through the entrance. "Besides, there are some new Solar Suits I want to…Oh no!" Kyla gasped in terror.

"What is it?" Ethel asked, "Weezliks?"

"Worse!" Kyla cried. "It's *her!* That big snob, Moli Neptune. She and her group think they're just the coolest kids on all nine planets."

She pointed to a group of girls who were standing near the entrance. In the center was a tall thin girl with long orange hair. "Hello, *Kyla,*" the orange-haired girl called in icy tones.

"Hello, *Moli,*" Kyla shot back.

"What's that you're wearing?" Moli asked. "It looks like it needs to be recycled."

All the other girls started to giggle.

"This is a disaster," Kyla whispered as she and Ethel walked toward the group. She looked down at the week-old jumpsuit she'd been wearing when they'd run out of the house. "My clothes are totally sub-orbital and my hair needs to be debugged. Just once I'd like to shut her up."

"Kyla," Ethel reminded her, "I think we have bigger problems than Moli Neptune."

"Oh yeah," Kyla replied sourly. "Like what?"

"Like the Weezliks my sensors have detected in the parking lot," Ethel tugged at her arm. "Come on! Escape is imperative!"

A wicked grin spread over Kyla's face. "I think I know a way to take care of Moli Neptune *and* the Weezliks at the same time!"

TO BE CONTINUED

LUNCH NOTES:

A REALLY BAD CYBER-HAIR DAY

DAY · 10 ·

"Kyla, come on!" Ethel whispered urgently. But Kyla ignored the robot and looked at Moli.

"You know, Moli, I think you're right," she said sweetly.

"You do?" Moli replied suspiciously.

"I just don't know how to dress myself," Kyla went on, a terribly sad expression on her face. "I wish I could be a total space fave like you."

"You do?" Moli repeated. Ethel tapped at Kyla's arm.

"You're about to be a total space *wreck*—let's go!" she whispered.

Kyla ignored her. Instead she gave Moli's clothes an envious look. Moli was wearing a jumpsuit that changed colors every three seconds.

"I wish I could dress just like you," Kyla sighed.

"This old thing?" Moli laughed, but sounded pleased

"Do you think…" said Kyla. "Could I use the clothes duplicator to copy it?"

"Sure," Moli sneered. "If you want."

Quickly, Kyla led Moli to a nearby duplicator booth.

"I'll just set this to make my clothes look exactly like yours," Kyla said, pressing a button. As she did, a robot voice boomed over the mall's loudspeakers:

"Attention, shoppers! Weezliks on level three. Please proceed to the nearest exit. And thank you for shopping at Astro Mall."

"Did you hear that?" Moli said as she stepped from the clothes duplicator. "I'm, like, out of here!" Then she looked down at herself. She turned to Kyla. "You…you…!" she gasped. "What did you do?"

CLOTHES DUPLICATOR

TO BE CONTINUED

LUNCH NOTES:

_____

_____

_____

_____

_____

_____

_____

A REALLY BAD CYBER-HAIR DAY

DAY · 11 ·

Kyla stepped out of the clothes duplicator wearing the same jumpsuit Moli had been wearing. And Moli looked like she was wearing Kyla's old "junksuit"—even her cyber hair. Kyla had reversed the controls!

"Bye, Moli," Kyla said as she ran away, followed by Ethel 417B.

"I'll get you for this!" Moli shouted.

"There she is!" cried a Weezlik voice. The Weezliks had entered the mall and they were heading straight for Moli!

"They think she's *you!*" said Ethel.

"Gee, isn't that too bad!" Kyla didn't sound the least bit sorry. "Don't worry, they'll let her go. I think. Where to now?"

"Why don't we call the Interstellar Landscaping and Defense Patrol?" Ethel suggested. "They're supposed to handle Weezlik problems."

"It's worth a try," replied Kyla, and she held up her wrist hyperlink. "Landscaping and Defense!" she commanded. Instantly a holograph image of a bored-looking woman in a gray uniform appeared next to them.

"Help!" Kyla shouted. "There are Weezliks after us! Their invasion plans are in my hair!"

"Weezliks?" the woman said, looking mildly surprised. "We thought they were still on vacation! You'd better get down to headquarters."

"Okay!" Kyla shouted. Luckily, they were standing near an entrance to a high speed transport tube. Kyla and Ethel jumped in and were whisked away like specks of dirt in a deep-space vacuum cleaner.

"I estimate 5.84 seconds until we arrive," Ethel said as they flew along.

"I sure hope..." Kyla started to say, when the tube and Ethel both disappeared.

TO BE CONTINUED

LUNCH BOX **DAY · 11 ·** LIBRARY

LUNCH NOTES:

THE STORY SO FAR...

Kyla was kidnapped on her way to headquarters.

A REALLY BAD CYBER-HAIR DAY

DAY 12

For a few seconds all Kyla could see were bright flashing lights. Then her vision cleared and she knew where she was—on the Weezlik invasion ship! They had beamed her up and strapped her to a table. Two Weezliks in white lab coats were attaching cables to her head.

"Hey! Watch the hair!" she snapped.

"Your hair is exactly what we're watching," said the croaking voice of Weezlik Commander Gerkin. He stepped into Kyla's view.

"You again?" Kyla said, trying to sound brave. "Why don't you quit?"

"Weezliks don't know the meaning of the word 'quit,'" he retorted.

"Then get a robo-dictionary," she said with a grim smile.

"Switching clothes and hair with that other human was very clever," the Weezlik went on.

"When we tried to download her hair, all we got were a bunch of video-phone numbers. The codes for the invasion must still be in *your* hair. We will soon find out. Unfortunately, the process may download some of your brains, too."

The Weezlik scientists began to roll Kyla toward an evil-looking machine covered with wires and long robotic arms.

"You lousy Weezlik!" Kyla shouted as she struggled to break free. "If my robo-tutor was here, she'd teach you a lesson!"

The Weezliks took the cables from Kyla's hair and quickly plugged them into the machine.

"This may hurt a bit," one of them said, and hit a button. Kyla's head began to ache.

"Help!" she screamed.

TO BE CONTINUED

LUNCH BOX · DAY 12 · LIBRARY

LUNCH NOTES:

THE STORY SO FAR...

The Weezliks captured Kyla and are about to download the invasion plans from her cyber hair.

A REALLY BAD CYBER-HAIR DAY

DAY 13

Kyla's head was spinning. The pain grew worse. She found herself thinking: "None of this would have happened if my parents had let me have my own Style-O-Matic."

Then she heard one of the Weezliks scream in fright.

At once, the pain vanished. Kyla's eyesight cleared. The Weezliks were all gathered around some sort of computer monitor, shouting and screeching in the strange Weezlik language. Then Commander Gerkin turned toward her. With a sharp claw, he lifted her from the table and carried her to the monitor.

"The hair codes!" he barked. "What did you do to your hair?"

"I changed styles with Moli," Kyla said innocently. "Do you like it?"

"You silly human!" he screeched.

"Your stupid hair codes put our computer into self-destruct mode! This ship will blow up in three minutes!"

"Gee," Kyla replied. "This really *is* a bad hair day!"

An ear-splitting alarm bell went off, and all the Weezliks scrambled for the nearest hatchway, clawing at each other to get out. Commander Gerkin shouted something at them, but they ignored him.

"Where are they going?" Kyla asked.

"To the escape pods!" Gerkin sneered as he strode after his fleeing crew. "I can't believe the entire Weezlik invasion is about to be destroyed by one human girl!"

"Hey, what about me?" Kyla cried as he left the room.

He turned, halfway through the hatch. "Sorry, I forgot," he said with an evil grin. "Have a nice day!"

> TO BE CONTINUED

LUNCH BOX **DAY** · 13 · LIBRARY

LUNCH NOTES:

THE STORY SO FAR...

The Weezliks abandoned Kyla after her hair codes put the ship on "self-destruct" mode.

A REALLY BAD CYBER-HAIR DAY

DAY 14

The alarm bells grew louder. A computer voice was talking.

"It must be the countdown until the ship blows up!" Kyla thought. "The commander mentioned escape pods! Maybe there's a spare!"

In a flash, she jumped through the hatch after the Weezliks and raced through the ship following the sound of Weezlik footsteps. As she turned one last corner she saw a Weezlik disappear into a hatch.

"There they are!" she thought. Her heart beat madly as she turned into the narrow steel corridor. "The escape pods! And there's one left!"

ZAAP!

A blast from a disrupter hit the wall just inches from her head. Kyla turned in fright. Had the Weezlik commander come back?

"Hi, *Kyla,*" a familiar voice sneered. "Going somewhere?"

It was Moli Neptune.

"Moli!" Kyla gasped breathlessly. "Come on! We only have a minute!"

"What do you mean *we?*" Moli said with a nasty grin.

"Aw, come on," Kyla said, trying to sound friendly. "You're not still mad, are you?"

"Why should I be mad?" Moli replied, pointing the sonic disrupter at Kyla's head. "Because you set me up to be kidnapped by Weezliks? Because they drained my brain? Because of these *icky clothes?*"

The computer voice was still counting in Weezlik.

"What's it saying?" Moli asked.

"I'm not sure," gulped Kyla. "But I think it's 10, 9, 8, 7, 6..."

TO BE CONTINUED

LUNCH BOX **DAY · 14 ·** LIBRARY

LUNCH NOTES:

_____

_____

_____

_____

_____

_____

_____

THE STORY SO FAR...

Moli and Kyla are left on the Weezlik ship as it's about to blow up.

A REALLY BAD CYBER-HAIR DAY

DAY · 15 ·

"5, 4, 3, 2..."

Kyla braced herself for the explosion that would blow her and Moli and the Weezlik ship into subatomic particles. But before the robot voice could say "1" in Weezlik, everything disappeared.

Colored lights flashed before her eyes. When her vision cleared, she was in a different place. Moli was standing next to her and right in front of them was...

"Ethel!" Kyla screamed with joy and jumped up. "What happened?"

Ethel patted Kyla. "Surely you didn't believe I was going to let Weezliks get my best pupil, did you? Not before final exams, anyway."

"But where...? How...?" Kyla asked.

A tall woman in a gray uniform stepped forward. "Welcome to the Interstellar Landscaping and Defense Patrol Headquarters," she said. "When the Weezliks beamed you aboard, we managed to get a transporter lock on you. We had to wait until you were near your friend Moli before we could beam you both down."

"Her *friend?*" Moli cried indignantly. "As *if.*"

The officer continued. "Thanks to you, Kyla, the Weezlik ship has been destroyed! You saved the planet!"

"Of course she's a hero," Ethel added. "After all, she has an excellent tutor." She turned to Kyla. "How does it feel to have saved humanity?"

"Pretty good," Kyla said, with a smile. "And you know what's even better?" she added as she looked at herself in a near-by holo-mirror. "I think that Weezlik computer did a really great job on my hair!"

THE END

LUNCH NOTES:

_____

_____

_____

_____

_____

_____

_____

THE MUMMY'S RING

Lee Brown hates snakes. Hugo North loves mummies. But with Pharaoh Pit-ptooey's ancient gold snake ring curled tightly around Lee's finger and the map of the Egyptian Museum stamped on Hugo's genius brain, the two are able to put their detective skills to the test and uncover a ruthless plot. Are snakes the scariest thing in the Museum? Read on and find out.

BY KATE MCMULLAN

"It's a copy of Pharaoh Pit-ptooey's ring, Lee," my friend Hugo told me.

Our class trip to the Egyptian Museum had just ended. Our teacher, Ms. de Pew, had given us ten minutes in the gift shop.

I pushed my glasses up on my nose as I studied the ring inside the little plastic box. It was shaped like a small gold snake curled in a circle, biting the tip of its tail. The snake had ruby-red eyes. But the ring was marked $4.95, so I knew they weren't *real* rubies.

"Not a bad copy, either," Hugo added.

My friend Hugo North may look like your average freckle-faced kid. But beneath his uncombed red hair lies the brain of a genius. Ancient Egypt is only one of his specialties.

I'm Lee Brown—brown eyes, brown hair. Hugo and I plan to open a detective agency together one day. My specialty is nerve. I am absolutely and totally fearless. Except for one thing.

"Why a snake ring, Lee?" Hugo said. "Snakes creep you out."

"Yeah, I know," I said. "But maybe this ring will help me get over that. Besides, I think it's sort of nice."

"Nice?" Hugo groaned. "Pharaoh Pit-ptooey's goldsmiths were the envy of the ancient world, and you call this *nice?*"

"Okay, maybe 'nice' isn't the word."

I stared at that little gold snake. I know it sounds silly, but his little ruby-red eyes seemed to stare right back at me. I felt a chill run down my spine.

TO BE CONTINUED

LUNCH BOX DAY ·1· LIBRARY

LUNCH NOTES:

_____

_____

_____

_____

_____

_____

_____

THE MUMMY'S RING

THE STORY SO FAR...

Lee was trying to decide whether to buy a snake ring in the Egyptian Museum gift shop.

"Line up, class!" Ms. de Pew called. "Our bus is here!"

I hurried over to the cash register with the ring.

"I'd like this ring, please," I told the woman behind the counter. Her name badge said *Rosetta Stone*. She had shoulder-length dark hair with bangs. She was thumbing through a magazine.

"You can't return it, so make sure it fits," Rosetta said, not even looking up from her magazine.

I snapped open the plastic box and took the ring out. It felt cold to the touch. I had my old pirate ring on my left hand, so I slid the snake ring onto the third finger of my right hand.

"Perfect," I said. "I'll take it."

Rosetta looked up then. When she saw the snake ring on my finger, she gasped.

I started to ask what was wrong, when Hugo appeared at my side. "Lee!" he cried. "Ms. de Pew's looking for you! I said I thought you were already on the bus, so come on!"

I shrugged Hugo off.

"What's the total with tax?" I asked Rosetta.

Still staring at the ring, she said, "Four hundred ninety-five thousand dollars."

TO BE CONTINUED

LUNCH BOX DAY · 2 · LIBRARY

LUNCH NOTES:

_____

_____

_____

_____

_____

_____

_____

THE MUMMY'S RING

DAY
· 3 ·

THE STORY SO FAR...

Lee had just been told that the snake ring costs almost half a million dollars.

I just couldn't believe what I'd heard! I pointed to the price sticker on the plastic box that had held the ring. "This says four dollars and ninety-five cents!"

"It's a mistake," Rosetta snapped.

"Lee!" Hugo waved frantically at the plate glass window. "The bus is leaving! Hurry!"

I glanced down at the little gold snake ring. I hated to take it off. But I didn't exactly have four hundred ninety-five thousand dollars in my wallet.

"Can I pay on the installment plan?" I joked.

Rosetta didn't crack a smile.

"Lee!" Hugo's face was turning bright red. "Let's go!"

"Okay!" I started to pull the ring off my finger. But no matter how I twisted, it refused to slide past my knuckle.

"It's stuck!" I whispered to Hugo.

He tried pulling on the ring.

"Ow!" I yanked my hand away. I turned to Rosetta. "I'm having a little trouble getting it off," I told her.

"Give me the ring—now!" she demanded.

"It's stuck!" I practically shouted. "What do you want me to do, cut off my finger?"

Rosetta reached out her own finger then. It had a long, red-polished nail at its tip. She pressed a button on the counter, and a shrill alarm bell started ringing.

"Guards!" she called. "Thief!"

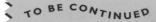
TO BE CONTINUED

LUNCH BOX **DAY · 3 ·** LIBRARY

LUNCH NOTES:

THE STORY SO FAR...

The woman in the gift shop called Lee a thief and set off the alarm.

THE MUMMY'S RING

DAY · 4 ·

For a moment, I stood frozen where I was. Then, without a word, Hugo and I ran out of the gift shop into the crowded museum lobby. We stopped, and I felt a cold hand on my shoulder. I whirled around, expecting to see a museum guard.

I found myself facing a skinny boy with a mouth full of braces. "Is this a fire drill?" he asked.

"No," I told him. "A jewel robbery."

I hurried off, following the blue-and-white picture signs to the rest room. Hugo followed me.

"I'm going to try to soap this thing off," I told Hugo, as the alarm bell finally stopped ringing. "Wait for me."

In the rest room, I stood at the sink and pushed the soap dispenser. Smelly pink soap squirted out onto my palm. I lathered up my hands. I tried to slip off the ring. It wouldn't slip.

I hit the soap dispenser again. A big blob of pink soap oozed out. I sudsed up my hands until they were really slippery. I worked the ring up to my knuckle. But it wouldn't come off.

My fingertips were starting to wrinkle. I squeezed my eyes shut and pulled on the ring with all my might. No luck.

With a sigh, I rinsed off the soap. I shook my hands to get the water off—and heard a *ping!* I glanced down in time to see the ring bounce off the edge of the sink.

I grabbed for it, but it disappeared down the drain.

TO BE CONTINUED

LUNCH NOTES:

THE MUMMY'S RING

DAY · 5 ·

"Darn it all!" I exclaimed. I'd always liked that old pirate ring. The snake ring was still curled tightly around my right ring finger. Pink soap was crusted around its ruby-red eyeballs.

"Any luck?" Hugo said when I came out of the bathroom.

I shook my head. "Maybe we should go back to the gift shop. I mean, I'm *not* trying to steal the ring." I glanced down at the little snake. "Hugo," I said, "you don't think this could really be the Pharaoh's ring, do you?"

Hugo took a long look. "You know, it looks real," he said. "But how could the Pharaoh's ring get into a plastic box in the gift shop?"

I didn't answer because just then a tall guard rounded the corner. I decided to do the right thing.

"I'm the one you're looking for." I stepped forward, holding up my hand to show the ring.

Then I gazed up at the tall guard's face. He looked just like a movie star—Boris Karloff in *Frankenstein!* When I showed him the ring, he shouted into his walkie-talkie. "I've got the suspect! By the first-floor rest room. Send backup! Hurry!"

"Hey, I'm turning myself in!" I protested, but he ignored me.

In seconds, more museum guards appeared. They ran at us from every direction. They circled us, stepping closer and closer.

The tall guard grinned, showing jagged teeth.

"Escape," he explained, "is impossible."

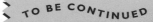

TO BE CONTINUED

LUNCH NOTES:

_____

_____

_____

_____

_____

_____

_____

THE MUMMY'S RING

DAY
· 6 ·

THE STORY SO FAR...

Lee and Hugo were surrounded by museum guards.

"Reach for the sky," the Frankenstein look-alike ordered.

"You're kidding, right?" I said. "Or have you seen way too many bad movies?"

"Lee, stop!" Hugo hissed. "You don't talk back to armed guards."

"Says who?" I hissed back. "You're way too obedient, Hugo. Anyway, they're only armed with walkie-talkies."

"No talking," the tall guard snapped. "Follow me."

He led us into a large elevator. Hugo and I got in, followed by all the guards. It was quite a squeeze. The tall guard pressed SB for sub-basement. The doors closed, and we started going down.

The elevator doors opened. The guard marched us down a hall and through a doorway marked DO NOT ENTER. We followed him along a passage to a second doorway marked ABSOLUTELY NO ENTRY. We walked through that to a closed door marked DON'T EVEN *THINK* ABOUT IT. The guard opened the door and shoved us through it. He slammed the door, locked it, and left us alone in the dark.

We sat down on the floor and waited. At last our eyes adjusted to the dark. We were able to see a little bit.

"We're in some sort of storage room," Hugo said.

We got up and began exploring. Shelves lined the walls, and on the shelves were. . .

"Mummies!" Hugo cried. "We're surrounded by mummies."

TO BE CONTINUED

LUNCH NOTES:

THE MUMMY'S RING

**DAY
· 7 ·**

"Oh, boy!" Hugo cried. He raced around, checking out the wrapped-up dead people. I'd rarely seen him so happy.

I sat back down and tried to think of an escape plan.

Hugo, meanwhile, knelt down beside one of the mummies. He poked around at it for a while, and I heard him muttering things like *This isn't right* and *That's strange.*

"What's wrong?" I called to him.

Hugo came over and sat down by me. "You know how the ancient Egyptians made mummies, right?"

I shook my head.

"Well, when someone died, embalmers laid the body on a stone table," Hugo said. "They made a cut in the left side of the abdomen and took out the liver and the lungs. They took out the brain, too. But they didn't cut open the skull. Instead, they stuck these long skinny sticks with little hooks on the end up the dead person's nose. . ."

"Okay, Hugo. I get the picture," I said.

But Hugo didn't even slow down. "They used the hooked sticks to mash up the brain," he told me, "and then they pulled it out in little pieces through the dead person's nose."

"Gross!" I shouted.

"Anyway," Hugo finally said, "what I'm trying to tell you is—these aren't real mummies! They're—"

But before Hugo could say another word, the door swung open.

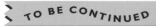

TO BE CONTINUED

LUNCH BOX **DAY · 7 ·** LIBRARY

LUNCH NOTES:

_____

_____

_____

_____

_____

_____

_____

THE MUMMY'S RING

Then someone flipped on a dim light. It was a big man with yellow hair and a yellow moustache. Next to him stood the tall guard.

"Good work, Karnac," the big man told the guard. Then he turned to me. "We must have the ring that you stole from—"

"But *I didn't* steal it!" I blurted out.

"Quiet!" the big man shouted.

"I only tried it on to see if it fit," I hurried on.

"QUIET!" the big man thundered.

"And now I can't get it off," I finished quickly.

"We'll get it off for you." The big man smiled, showing big, yellow teeth. He turned to the guard. "Karnac?"

Karnac stepped forward. He held a pair of wire cutters.

"Hold out your right hand," the big guy ordered.

"Good idea." I held out my hand, palm up. "Snip it off."

"What?" The big man's face grew angry. "Cut a priceless, 3,500-year-old ring?" he shouted. "I don't think so!"

I drew back my hand. "Maybe we should discuss this."

Karnac opened the wire cutters wider. It was pretty clear what he had in mind.

"Hold out your right hand," the man ordered again.

Karnac stepped closer. He nosed the wire cutters around my finger, just below the ring. Then he started to squeeze.

"Hey, look!" Hugo yelled suddenly, pointing toward the dark back part of the room. "That mummy! It—it's moving!"

TO BE CONTINUED

LUNCH BOX DAY ·8· LIBRARY

LUNCH NOTES:

_____

_____

_____

_____

_____

_____

_____

THE MUMMY'S RING

THE STORY SO FAR...

The tall guard, Karnac, had a pair of wire cutters when Hugo yelled that a mummy was moving.

The two men whirled around, staring into the darkness.

By the time they'd turned back to us, I'd yanked my finger away and Hugo and I had bolted.

"Nice work, Hugo," I called as we zoomed out the door. We sped down a dimly lit hallway. "But now we're lost!"

"Not really," Hugo called back. "I have a book at home with a map of this whole museum. I know exactly where we are."

I heard Karnac running behind us. We put on more speed. We raced around a corner and saw an elevator! It was our only hope. I glanced over my shoulder. Karnac was gaining on us!

Hugo reached the elevator first. He pressed the call button. The doors stayed closed.

He pressed it again. Nothing happened.

Karnac was getting closer.

Hugo punched the button again. The doors parted. We ran inside. Hugo pressed DOOR CLOSE. Nothing happened.

Karnac kept racing towards us.

Hugo and I pushed on the doors, trying to make them close faster. Slowly they began to close.

"Hold the door." Karnac cried. He put out an arm and lunged. The last thing I saw were his fingertips as the elevator doors thudded shut. "Hugo!" I shouted. "We're saved!"

"Not really," Hugo said.

Then I saw what he meant.

There was a sign inside the elevator. It said: OUT OF ORDER.

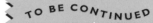

TO BE CONTINUED

LUNCH BOX **DAY 9** LIBRARY

LUNCH NOTES:

_____

_____

_____

_____

_____

_____

_____

THE STORY
SO FAR...

Hugo and Lee had
escaped Karnac
only to find them-
selves in a broken
elevator.

THE MUMMY'S RING

"No! It can't be broken!" I yelled. I slammed the heel of my hand angrily into the elevator buttons. "Ow!" I cried.

The elevator jolted and started going up. Hugo pressed the 4 button.

"Mummies are on 4," he said. "I have to check something."

"What?" I cried. "I'm being chased by a guard trying to turn me into a nine-fingered wonder, and you want to do *research?*"

Hugo shrugged. The elevator shuddered to a stop on 4. We stepped out into a darkened gallery. The only light came from the exit signs over the fire doors. We scurried through hallways like rats, darting from doorway to doorway. At last we came to a room filled with mummy coffins. Hugo led the way to the smallest one.

"Pharaoh Pit-ptooey's mummy is inside here," he whispered.

"But it's so small," I whispered back.

"He died when he was only seven," Hugo reminded me. "The snake ring you're wearing is small, too. That's another reason I think it's real. It wouldn't make sense for a gift-shop copy to be that little. It wouldn't fit anyone."

Hugo walked over to a glass case. "Lee, look!" he said. "It's the same snake ring! I have to get it out of here!"

"Are you crazy?" I said. "You'll set off an alarm!"

Hugo shook his head. "I've read how pros do this," he told me. Then he took a piece of wire from his pocket and began wiggling it between the pieces of glass in the display case.

Instantly, an alarm started blaring right over our heads!

TO BE CONTINUED

LUNCH NOTES:

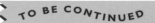

THE MUMMY'S RING

DAY · 11 ·

THE STORY SO FAR...

Hugo had just opened a glass case of Pharaoh Pit-ptooey's jewelry and set off the museum alarm.

"Let's go, Hugo!" I yelled over the alarm. "It's not a good idea to be found at the crime scene!"

"We need proof," he said. Then he pushed up—*hard*—on the top of the display case. The case opened. Hugo snatched the ring and a bracelet and slipped them into his pocket. Then we ran from the room and down a wide hallway. When I stopped, I heard someone running after us. And I knew Karnac was on the 4th floor.

"Look! Over there!" I ran over to a small counter where posters were sold. The back of the counter was hollow. We ducked under it, out of sight. We held still. We hardly breathed. The footsteps grew louder and louder. The floor trembled with each step Karnac took. Then the footsteps faded. Karnac was running away from us. It seemed too good to be true! When we couldn't hear any footsteps, Hugo and I crawled out from our hiding place. Hugo pointed to some blue-and-white picture symbols for *man, woman* and *telephone*. It was pretty clear which one we needed.

We crept along the shadowy hallways to the phone. There it hung, on the wall, a big, black, beautiful box. Hugo picked up the receiver and put it to his ear. He punched in 911, the police emergency number. "Hello?" he whispered hoarsely. "I'm calling from the. . ."

"Drop the phone!" Karnac's voice boomed behind us. "Now!"

TO BE CONTINUED

LUNCH BOX **DAY · 11 ·** LIBRARY

LUNCH NOTES:

_____

_____

_____

_____

_____

_____

_____

THE MUMMY'S RING

THE STORY SO FAR...

Hugo had just dialed the police when Karnac demanded that he drop the phone.

Good old obedient Hugo. He did as he was told.

Karnac grabbed me and snapped cold metal cuffs on my wrists.

"Stop it!" Hugo yelled. "You're a guard here at the Egyptian Museum on Metro Boulevard! You're here to guard treasures!" Hugo raved on. "Not beat up kids, such as Lee Brown and me—Hugo North! We came here with Ms. de Pew and our class from P.S. 16, and you've taken us prisoner! We need help!"

Hugo ranted like a maniac. I knew that delicate genius brain of his had blown its fuse. When Karnac came at him with a pair of handcuffs, Hugo simply held his hands out. It was embarrassing.

Karnac gave us another elevator ride, and we ended up back in the gift shop. Rosetta was waiting for us. "Take the one with the ring over there," she said, pointing to a far corner of the gift shop. "I don't want to make a mess by the cash register."

"Oh, great!" I cried. "I'm about to get my finger cut off, and you're worried about not making a mess?"

"Cutting off fingers is not my style," Rosetta declared. "If that ring went *on* over your knuckle, it can come *off* over your knuckle. And I have just what we need to make that happen. The oiliest, slipperiest, greasiest thing in the world."

"Major Mike's Fried Chicken?" Karnac asked eagerly.

"No," said Rosetta. "Something even greasier."

She opened a drawer and lifted out a small wooden cage.

TO BE CONTINUED

LUNCH BOX **DAY 12** LIBRARY

LUNCH NOTES:

THE MUMMY'S RING

DAY · 13 ·

THE STORY SO FAR...

Rosetta had just picked up a small cage with the oiliest, greasiest thing in the world inside.

Coiled on the bottom of the cage was a little green snake.

"This is *Slippiricus vipericus,*" Rosetta said proudly. "Better known as the 'slippery viper' or 'the oil-slick viper.' Or simply 'the disgusting little snake.'" She opened the cage door. The snake poked its head out. It sniffed the air with its tiny forked tongue and slithered out of its cage.

"Gross!" Hugo cried as the snake's odor filled the room.

"Ugh!" I gagged. "That smells disgusting! And what does the stinking snake have to do with getting the ring off anyway?"

"All you have to do is let it curl around your finger," Rosetta explained. "Once it feels comfortable, it will ooze a little snake oil. The ring of Pharaoh Pit-ptooey will slide off your finger." She smiled. "Now, hold out your hand."

I eyed that foul snake. "I vote for wire cutters," I said.

Rosetta only sneered. "Your hand!"

I drew a breath. I was fearless, right? My fingers hardly quivered at all as I held out both my hands, cuffed together as they were, and put them on the counter. The snake crept toward me, closer and closer. But when it was only inches away, I started shaking. I must have measured 9.9 on the Richter scale.

"Stop shaking!" Rosetta hissed. "You'll scare my viper! And it's never a good idea to frighten a deadly poisonous snake."

TO BE CONTINUED

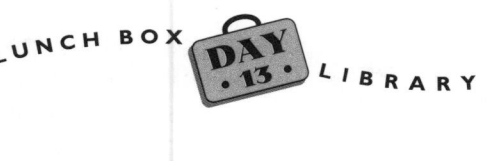

LUNCH BOX **DAY · 13 ·** LIBRARY

LUNCH NOTES:

THE MUMMY'S RING

DAY · 14 ·

THE STORY SO FAR...

A deadly poisonous snake was about to slither onto Lee's ring finger.

I stopped shaking. The snake crept closer. Its awful stench made my eyes water and my nose tickle. I felt a sneeze coming on . . . AH-CHOOOO! I blew that viper halfway across the room.

"Oh, my snake!" Rosetta cried.

"Freeze!" a voice called from the doorway. A man and a woman in police uniforms stood there with their guns drawn.

Now it was Rosetta and Karnac's turn to reach for the sky.

"How did you know we were here?" I asked the policeman.

"The 911 phone call," he said as he unlocked my cuffs.

Hugo smiled. "I dropped the receiver, but I never hung up."

"So *that's* why you were yelling that strange stuff," I said.

"Thanks to you," the policewoman said, "we nailed Rosetta's gang. We couldn't arrest them until we knew their scam."

"Their scam," Hugo piped up, "was stealing real jewelry and shipping it out of the museum wrapped up in phony mummies. They put cheap, gift-shop copies of the jewelry on display." He held up the Pharaoh's bracelet. "This is from a case on the fourth floor. It's plastic!" He gave it to the policeman. "But things got mixed up," Hugo went on, "and Pharaoh Pit-ptooey's real ring got put into a gift-shop box by mistake."

"You blew it, Karnac!" Rosetta cried. "Now we're finished!"

"Not quite," said a voice from the door.

It was the big, yellow-mustached guy. He was holding a gun. "Reach for the moon," he told the police. They did.

TO BE CONTINUED

LUNCH BOX **DAY · 14 ·** LIBRARY

LUNCH NOTES:

THE MUMMY'S RING

THE STORY SO FAR...

The police had just rescued them when Rosetta's game turned the tables.

Rosetta started hunting for her snake. Karnac handcuffed the police. Hugo made a break for the door. The big man lunged after him. I saw that the little green snake had crawled back into its cage. I picked up the cage and crept up behind the big man. I opened the cage and, with a pencil, picked up the viper. I put it to the big man's neck and yelled, "Reach for the stars!" He did.

After that, more cops came and took Rosetta and her gang away. I got the snake back into its cage, and realized I wasn't afraid of it. I even said I'd take it to the zoo the next day. Then Hugo and I slid into the back seat of the squad car. The policewoman said, "We got a bucket of Major Mike's Fried Chicken for our dinner." She handed it to us. "Here, have some."

All I did was pick up a drumstick, and the Pharaoh's ring slid off my finger. I handed it to the policewoman. Hugo gave her the ring from the display case. But she had greasy fingers, too, and she dropped them. "Oops!" she said. "Uh-oh. Which is which?"

She handed them to Hugo. "This one's real," he said. He gave that one to the policewoman. Then he handed the other one to me.

"But this is the one I had on all the time!" I exclaimed. "Look, there's the pink soap stuck around its ruby eyeball."

"Wow," said Hugo. "This ring deserves a place in the *Guinness Book of World Records* as the Greatest Fake of All Time."

I slipped the ring on. Maybe it was the 3,500-year-old Pit-ptooey ring. Maybe Hugo's was the fake. Who knew? All I knew was that thanks to that little gold snake, I was now 100% fearless!

THE END

LUNCH BOX DAY · 15 · LIBRARY

LUNCH NOTES:

CREAMPUFF, THE HEROIC HAMSTER

You don't think a hamster can be a hero? Meet Creampuff, who risks drowning, battles dangerous insects, leaps from enormous heights, and survives the garbage can, all for the love of Daphne. As he escapes 48 giant feet, defeats the school cafeteria, solves a mystery, and saves the day, Creampuff proves he's the biggest little hero he's ever met.

BY RICHIE CHEVAT

CREAMPUFF, THE HEROIC HAMSTER

"Just a little more, just a little more, just a little more…" Creampuff knew he couldn't quit. He had to keep going, no matter how much his legs screamed in pain, no matter how his lungs ached with every breath. Over and over he forced himself to reach up and grab another rung of the spinning metal wheel.

"Why do I do it?" he asked himself for the hundredth time. But he already knew the answer. *"Because I'm a hamster, that's why."*

"Got to keep going, got to keep going," he told himself as the metal wheel spun noisily. *"Daphne is counting on me."*

Daphne was Creampuff's ten-year-old owner. She was the reason he ran around in his wheel for hours at a time. He didn't know why she wanted him to do it, but after all, she had put the wheel in his cage so it must be important. And he wasn't about to let her down.

"Can't quit, can't quit," he repeated to himself. *"Can't…"*

Suddenly, the entire cage shook like a herd of elephants were doing the mambo in Daphne's bedroom. Creampuff was thrown from the wheel and landed on his back in a pile of sawdust.

"Earthquake!" he thought as the cage floor tilted wildly from side to side. *"It's an earthquake! Grab your sunflower seeds and head for the hills!"*

TO BE CONTINUED

LUNCH BOX  LIBRARY

LUNCH NOTES:

CREAMPUFF, THE HEROIC HAMSTER

THE STORY SO FAR...

Creampuff was taking his daily run when a huge earthquake knocked him off his feet.

"Got to get up, got to save Daphne!" Creampuff thought as the cage floor heaved up and down. With a mighty effort he rolled to his feet and scrambled toward the cage door.

And then suddenly the earthquake stopped. Daphne's round face appeared next to the cage bars.

"Sorry about that, Creampuff," the little girl said, as she picked up the cage from where she had dropped it. "I slipped."

Then she added, "You're going to Show and Tell today."

"Show and Tell?" thought Creampuff. *"Sounds dangerous. Good thing you're bringing me along."*

In the kitchen, Creampuff was knocked off his feet again as Daphne dropped the cage onto the table with a thud. A few seconds later he heard the cage door open and a huge hand reached in and grabbed him.

"Oh good," he thought as he was lifted through the air. *"Daphne wants to play."*

But with a shock, he saw that it wasn't Daphne at all—it was Tommy, Daphne's little brother!

"Hey, Creampuff," the six-year-old said merrily as he held the struggling hamster close to his face. "Want to go for a swim?"

He lowered the helpless hamster toward the kitchen sink, which was brimming with soapy water and dirty dishes.

"But I don't know how to swim!" thought Creampuff as the dark, dirty water drew closer and closer. *"I'm going to drown!"*

TO BE CONTINUED

LUNCH BOX **DAY · 2 ·** LIBRARY

LUNCH NOTES:

_____

_____

_____

_____

_____

_____

_____

THE STORY SO FAR...

Daphne's brother, Tommy, thought it would be fun if Creampuff went for a swim.

CREAMPUFF, THE HEROIC HAMSTER

DAY · 3 ·

"Tommy, you put that hamster back right now!"

Creampuff's rear paws were an inch from the water.

"Aw, Mom, I wasn't going to hurt him."

"I know, dear," his mom said. "But sometimes you're not careful."

Tommy gently placed Creampuff back in his cage.

"Something tells me I haven't seen the last of him," the hamster thought as he curled up in a corner.

He must have dozed off, because he was awakened by the sound of a car door slamming shut. He was on the back seat of the family car, with Daphne next to him.

"Are you excited about the play, dear?" Daphne's mom asked, as the car sped along.

"Yeah!" Daphne answered. "Wait till you see the costumes! We've been working on them for a month."

The car turned a corner and Creampuff was thrown against his food dish. A bump in the road sent him flying backward.

"Got to hold on!" he thought.

A terrible buzzing noise filled his ears. Creampuff sniffed the air, alert for danger. What was it? Was it Tommy again?

And then he saw it—black and yellow stripes, rushing wings, a long deadly stinger. A bumblebee had gotten inside Creampuff's cage!

The small rodent felt his fur bristle with anger. He couldn't let that bee sting Daphne. Bravely, he drew himself up and planted his paws firmly in the sawdust.

"You're not getting past me, buzz brain," he thought grimly as he prepared for the fight of his life.

TO BE CONTINUED

LUNCH BOX DAY · 3 · LIBRARY

LUNCH NOTES:

THE STORY SO FAR...

Creampuff must do battle with a giant bumblebee who's invaded his cage.

CREAMPUFF, THE HEROIC HAMSTER

"Come on, pollen breath," Creampuff sneered, as he braced himself for the bee's deadly attack.

"Boy, is it hot in here," said Daphne at the same moment and rolled down her window. A gust of air blew through the car and whisked the bee outside.

"Guess he wasn't as tough as he looked," Creampuff gloated. For the rest of the trip he stood guard, but the bee never returned.

Soon Creampuff found himself in Daphne's classroom.

"I guess I am pretty special," he thought proudly as Daphne took him out and held him up for everyone to see.

"Does he do any tricks?" asked one of the boys.

"Tricks?" Creampuff sniffed. *"What do I look like, a German shepherd? Tell him, Daphne."*

But before Daphne could say anything, a loud adult voice interrupted. It was Ms. Wilson, Daphne's teacher.

"Children, I have some bad news," she said with a frown. "We can't find the box with costumes for our class play, *Charlotte's Web.* If we can't find them by tonight, I don't know what we're going to do."

"The costumes!" Daphne cried. Creampuff's heart sank when he saw the look of dismay on her face.

"Poor Daphne," he thought as she placed him back in his cage. *"I bet I could find those costumes. If only I could…"*

Creampuff froze in mid-thought, his eyes glued to the cage door. In the excitement over the costumes, Daphne had forgotten to latch it!

TO BE CONTINUED

LUNCH NOTES:

CREAMPUFF, THE HEROIC HAMSTER

THE STORY SO FAR...

The class play costumes are missing, and Daphne forgot to latch Creampuff's cage door.

Creampuff ran to the door and looked out. Ms. Wilson and the class had forgotten about him. He stopped for a brief moment. What would Daphne think if he left the cage on his own? Then he remembered the missing costumes and the look on Daphne's face.

"This is a job for Creampuff!" he told himself and bravely nosed the door aside.

The cage was sitting on top of a wide bookshelf. To Creampuff it was like the edge of the Grand Canyon.

"Better get back in your cage," said a strange voice. Creampuff jumped in fright. A giant, the biggest hamster in the world, was talking to him from a glass tank on the same bookshelf. Then he realized it wasn't a hamster at all, but the class guinea pig, Spot.

"I'm going to go find the costumes!" Creampuff announced.

The guinea pig looked at him curiously. "But you're just a hamster," he observed.

"Just a hamster?" Creampuff replied angrily. "A lot you know. I'm *Creampuff!"* And he turned his back and stalked off.

Following the edge, he came to a long, wooden block. Like a bridge, it stretched from that bookcase to another a couple of feet away.

"This might be the way down," Creampuff thought. One paw at a time, he began to edge his way across the dizzying heights. Without warning, one of his rear feet slipped off the block! Desperately he grabbed on with his front paws as he slipped further.

"Got to hold on," he thought as he dangled over the terrifying drop. *"If I hit that floor, I'll be a hamster pancake!"*

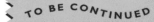
TO BE CONTINUED

LUNCH BOX  LIBRARY

LUNCH NOTES:

_____

_____

_____

_____

_____

_____

_____

CREAMPUFF, THE HEROIC HAMSTER

THE STORY SO FAR...

Creampuff lost his balance on top of a bookcase and is dangling by his front feet.

The classroom floor looked a hundred miles away. Only Creampuff's front claws kept him from plunging to his doom. With a mighty effort, he dug into the wooden block and heaved until his rear feet could catch hold. For a moment he lay there, exhausted. Then he began crawling forward.

At the far end of the bridge was another bookcase, filled with more blocks. Luckily, they hadn't been put away very neatly, just piled up in a heap, so it was easy for Creampuff to find his way down to the floor by jumping from one block to another.

"I did it!" he thought as he hopped onto the carpet. *"Now, where are those costumes?"*

On all sides the students' desks towered above him like skyscrapers. The students'

legs were like giant tree trunks.

"Hmm," the brave hamster thought, spying a crack under the door. *"I bet I can squeeze through there."*

He trotted for the closed door.

"Almost there," he thought with relief. *"Just a few more feet."*

RING!!!

A hammering bell shook the entire room. In a flash, two dozen students jumped to their feet. Desk tops slammed, books crashed to the floor like giant boulders. Creampuff stood frozen to the spot as four dozen feet rumbled across the floor like a herd of buffalo. And they were all headed straight for the door—straight for him! It was then that he heard Ms. Wilson say that terrible word:

"Recess!"

TO BE CONTINUED

LUNCH BOX **DAY · 6 ·** LIBRARY

LUNCH NOTES:

CREAMPUFF, THE HEROIC HAMSTER

THE STORY SO FAR...

The bell for recess rang, sending 48 running feet stampeding right for Creampuff.

The trampling

feet came closer and closer. In another few seconds Creampuff would be squashed. It was too late to reach the door. But just a few inches away was Ms. Wilson's tote bag, lying on its side. With a burst of speed, the little hamster ran for the safety of the bag and whisked inside.

"That was close," he sighed as the herd of feet rushed past and out the door. At the same moment, he heard Ms. Wilson's booming voice.

"Time for lunch," she cried happily and grabbed the tote bag handles.

"Whoa!" Creampuff slid downward into the bottom of the bag.

"Ouch!" A pencil fell over and hit him in the head.

"Yeow!" A heavy notebook was thrown sideways, pinning him against the hard, round side of a thermos. He managed to squeeze out from underneath.

The bag swung wildly through the air. Creampuff grew dizzier and dizzier. He started to be sick. And then he smelled it.

"What is that?" he wondered, whipping his small body around and looking in all directions. *"It smells like something dead and horrible. And it's IN HERE WITH ME!"*

The smell was growing worse every second. It was coming from a brown paper bag behind the thermos.

"It'll take more than a little smell to stop me!" Creampuff thought.

Carefully, with every nerve alert, he crept toward the brown paper bag.

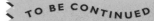

TO BE CONTINUED

LUNCH BOX **DAY · 7 ·** LIBRARY

LUNCH NOTES:

CREAMPUFF, THE HEROIC HAMSTER DAY ·8·

THE STORY SO FAR...

Creampuff noticed a disgusting stench coming from a small paper bag.

"Ugh!" As Creampuff poked his nose into the open bag, the smell was overpowering. Every instinct in his little hamster body told him to turn and run. But bravely, he forced himself inside.

There it was—a large square-sided object made up of several layers. The top and the bottom were a dark brown. In the middle were some bright yellow slabs and some stuff that was a sickening pink color. A yellow ooze flowed out from between the different layers. It was the pink stuff that smelled the worst.

"It's some kind of POISON!" Creampuff realized with a shudder.

THUD!

The tote bag stopped its swinging and landed on something hard. Through the bag he could hear Ms. Wilson's voice.

"Any news about the missing costumes?" she asked. Creampuff couldn't make out the reply.

"Too bad," Ms. Wilson said a moment later. "Maybe they'll turn up. Well, it's time for lunch."

Creampuff heard a rustling and suddenly felt the paper bag rising through the air like an elevator. Ms. Wilson had taken it out of the tote bag and he was still inside, trapped with the poisonous mess! He scrambled to hide, but the only thing he could manage was to shove his nose under the disgusting heap.

"Mmm, I'm so hungry I could eat a horse," Ms. Wilson said as she reached into the bag.

TO BE CONTINUED

LUNCH NOTES:

_____

_____

_____

_____

_____

_____

_____

THE STORY SO FAR...

Creampuff was still inside the bag when Ms. Wilson reached into it for her lunch.

CREAMPUFF, THE HEROIC HAMSTER · DAY · 9 ·

"Aaah!!"

Ms. Wilson screamed in fright and dropped the bag. Luckily, the soft brown smelly thing cushioned Creampuff's fall. He quickly scooted for the nearest wall.

"There was a mouse on my salami sandwich!" Ms. Wilson yelled.

"A sandwich?" Creampuff thought, as he squeezed under a nearby door, *"I'll remember to avoid those in the future!"*

Once on the other side he stopped and looked around. The air was filled with strange smells and the clang of pots and pans. People rushed back and forth. It was the cafeteria kitchen. And there, by a long metal counter, was a pile of boxes.

"Hmm, maybe the costumes are in one of those," he thought, gazing up at the tall tower of boxes. *"It'll be a long climb, but I can do it —for Daphne!"* With a mighty effort, he pulled himself up the side until he reached the counter top. Then he looked down into the top box.

"Lettuce!" he said to himself when he saw the leafy green heads. *"That reminds me, I haven't had lunch yet!"*

And then the counter top began to lurch and vibrate. Creampuff turned quickly and what he saw made his blood freeze. The counter top was really a wide black belt that was moving steadily toward a dark, square doorway in a huge machine. Hot blasts of steam and horrible noises came out of the door. And every second, the belt was dragging him closer and closer to the mouth of the hideous beast.

"Oh, no!" Creampuff thought in horror. *"A hamster-eating monster!"*

TO BE CONTINUED

LUNCH BOX  LIBRARY

DAY·9·

LUNCH NOTES:

THE STORY SO FAR...

A hamster-eating monster in the cafeteria is dragging Creampuff into its mouth.

"I'm too young to die!" thought Creampuff. He ran, but the deadly doorway drew closer. Suddenly he realized, *"I have to run to the side."* At the last moment, he leaped off the belt and landed on the lid of a plastic garbage can.

"Hey, Joe, turn off the dishwasher!" he heard someone yell as he slid to the floor. "I thought I saw something moving."

"A dishwasher?" Creampuff said to himself as he sped away. *"Why would a monster want to wash dishes?"*

He ran through an open doorway, right into the school cafeteria.

"Hey, it's a rat!" a boy yelled at the top of his lungs.

"A rat?" Creampuff thought. *"How rude!"*

The cafeteria went crazy. Half the kids were screaming "Rat!" and jumping on their tables and the other half were trying to catch him. But he was too quick.

"It'll take more than a bunch of screaming kids to catch me," Creampuff gloated as he slipped through a pair of snatching hands, ran around a chair and dived into an empty paper bag.

"They'll never find me in here," he thought. Then he heard a very familiar voice.

"Creampuff! Creampuff!" It was Daphne! And from the sound of her voice, she was in trouble.

"I'm coming, Daphne! Hold on!"

Creampuff was set to spring out of the bag and go to Daphne's rescue when someone picked up the bag and carried it away. With a sinking heart, he heard Daphne's voice fade in the distance.

"Creampuff… Creeeeampuuuuuff…"

TO BE CONTINUED

LUNCH NOTES:

_____

_____

_____

_____

_____

_____

_____

CREAMPUFF, THE HEROIC HAMSTER

THE STORY SO FAR...

Someone just picked up and carried away the paper bag where Creampuff was hiding.

"I've got to get out of here," Creampuff thought as he bounced around in the bag, *"Daphne needs me!"*

But before he could come up with an escape plan, the paper bag he was riding in was thrown through the air. Creampuff was turned head over heels several times as he and the bag rose and dropped like a roller coaster. With a tremendous shock he fell on something.

"Where am I?" he wondered as he cautiously poked his nose out of the bag. He was on a mound of food—wonderful, delicious food! There was lettuce and peas and carrots and apples and much more all mixed together. His mouth watered at the sight of it all.

"I'm starving," the hamster realized. He crawled toward an appetizing clump of peaches in syrup, when he heard a loud voice.

"Look at all this garbage!" a man was saying. "Better take it to the trash compactor."

"Garbage?" Creampuff wondered as he began to nibble. *"I don't see any garbage."*

He looked up and caught a glimpse of a middle-aged man reaching down. Creampuff braced himself for a fight, but the man didn't even notice him. Instead, he grabbed the edges of the plastic trash bag and quickly tied them together. Creampuff was in the dark. He felt the bag being lifted up.

"Compactor?" mused Creampuff. *"Sounds like another name for a hamster cage!"*

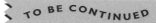

LUNCH BOX DAY · 11 · LIBRARY

LUNCH NOTES:

CREAMPUFF, THE HEROIC HAMSTER

DAY 12

THE STORY SO FAR...

Creampuff was heading toward a trash compactor. Was that another name for a hamster cage?

"I can't hang around in here all day," thought Creampuff. *"I've got costumes to find!"* In a flash, he crawled over the mounds of garbage to the soft black wall of the trash bag. With his sharp teeth he ripped a hole in the plastic.

"Ha!" he thought as he poked his head through the hole. *"They haven't made the bag that can hold Creampuff the hamster!"*

The bag swung back and forth as the custodian carried it down the school hallway. As Creampuff squeezed himself through the jagged hole, the rip began to widen. With a crash, the bottom of the bag tore open, scattering the trash over the floor and Creampuff with it.

"Freedom!" Creampuff thought as he scurried down the hall. He saw an open door and dashed through into a large closet. Right in the middle of the floor was a large cardboard box.

"Hmm, maybe there's more lettuce," he thought as he crawled up the side. But when he looked down, he saw the grinning face of a huge red fox! With lightning reflexes, Creampuff turned to leap away, but his claw slipped and he fell right into the gaping jaws!

"Tell Daphne I went out like a true hamster!" he thought as he waited for the fox's fangs to close over him. Nothing happened. Slowly Creampuff looked around. There were other animal faces all around him—cows, sheep, chickens.

"This isn't a real fox," he realized. *"It's one of the costumes! I did it! I found the costumes!"*

"Ha! I found you!" said a very familiar voice at the same moment.

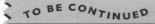

TO BE CONTINUED

LUNCH BOX **DAY · 12 ·** LIBRARY

LUNCH NOTES:

THE STORY SO FAR...

Creampuff found the costumes just before someone with a familiar voice found Creampuff.

CREAMPUFF, THE HEROIC HAMSTER

DAY . 13 .

Creampuff was seized by a huge hand and lifted into the air. What he saw made him shudder with fear. The person who had caught him was none other than his enemy, Tommy!

"Tommy? Not Tommy!" Creampuff thought. *"And just when I found the costumes! Is there no justice?"*

"Hey, hold still, little guy," Tommy said with a friendly smile. "I only want to help you."

"Yeah, right," Creampuff scoffed as Tommy carried him out of the closet. *"That's what you always say."* Then he added, *"I hate it when he calls me 'little guy.'"*

Tommy tenderly examined the little hamster.

"I'll show Mom I can be careful when I take care of you," the boy said. His face brightened. "I know, I'll give you a bath!"

"A bath? Hamsters never take baths!" Creampuff struggled as Tommy carried him into a nearby bathroom. He held Creampuff over a sink and began to fill it up with water.

"Oh, we need something to dry you off with," the boy said. "How about toilet paper?"

Tommy went to the toilet and tried to tear off some toilet paper with his free hand. The paper shredded into strips.

"This is no good," Tommy said as he threw the ripped paper into the toilet and flushed it. The roar of the rushing water sounded like Niagara Falls. At that very instant, Tommy loosened his grip just a bit and Creampuff slipped out. As the rodent hero fell, all he could see was the gaping whirlpool of water disappearing down the drain. *"Oh no!"* he thought as he dropped. *"I'm going to be flushed!"*

TO BE CONTINUED

LUNCH NOTES:

_____

_____

_____

_____

_____

_____

_____

CREAMPUFF, THE HEROIC HAMSTER DAY · 14 ·

THE STORY SO FAR...

Creampuff escaped Tommy's clutches, but he's falling straight into a flushing toilet.

With a thud, Creampuff hit the toilet seat and bounced onto the floor.

"Creampuff!" Tommy shouted in real horror. "Did I flush you?"

"Not this time, Buster!" Creampuff thought. He rolled onto his feet and started to run.

The little hamster ran for his life. And for something else—he had to find those costumes again. He got to the door just a few seconds ahead of the boy and darted down the hall.

"I think the closet was this way," he thought. He scooted inside the open door and ran right for the cardboard box. He heard Tommy shouting in the hallway.

"Creampuff, come back!"

"Almost there!" he thought as he scrambled up the side of the box. It was too late! The closet door opened and someone stepped inside and reached for him. It was Daphne!

"There you are, Creampuff," she cried. "I've been looking everywhere for you."

"Daphne!" Creampuff's heart leapt with joy. *"I did it! I led Daphne to the costumes!"*

But just as suddenly his heart sank like a stone. Without looking, Daphne turned around and started to leave the closet. She hadn't seen the costumes!

"Daphne! The costumes! They're here!"

It was no use. She was leaving the costumes behind. And there was nothing he could do about it!

TO BE CONTINUED

DAY
· 14 ·

LUNCH NOTES:
_____
_____
_____
_____
_____
_____
_____

CREAMPUFF, THE HEROIC HAMSTER

THE STORY SO FAR...

Daphne was standing right in front of the costumes, but she didn't notice them!

"Daphne, turn around! The costumes!" It was no use; he just couldn't make Daphne understand.

Creampuff looked down and saw the costume box below him. He knew this was his last chance. In another moment, she would walk out of there. Taking a deep breath, he did the only thing he could think of—he bit her!

"Creampuff!" Daphne screeched and dropped him—right into the open box.

"Sorry, Daphne," he thought as he landed on a large pair of bunny ears. *"But it was for your own good."*

"Creampuff!" Daphne said, still angry. "You never did that before. What …" And then she stopped. "The costumes," she whispered. Then she repeated it, at the top of her lungs. "THE COSTUMES!" Her shouting brought a crowd of people to the door of the closet.

"This is wonderful," said Ms. Wilson when she saw the box. "Good work, Daphne."

"It wasn't me," Daphne said, holding her hamster up for everyone to see. "It was my hamster."

"Aw, how could a hamster find the costumes?" asked one of the boys in her class.

"He isn't just a hamster," Daphne said with pride. "He's Creampuff! Creampuff the hero!"

"That's right!" Creampuff thought with pride. *"Defender of the weak, finder of costumes, eater of lettuce! Wherever there is injustice in this world, you'll find me (as long as my cage door is open). Because I'm Creampuff, the Heroic Hamster!"*

> THE END

LUNCH NOTES:

SARAH ZODD'S ARABIAN NIGHTS

Sarah Zodd isn't exactly the literary type, but she's smack in the middle of her very own Arabian nightmare, thanks to a magic lamp and a friend with a sore throat. She may hate public speaking, but she'll have to think fast and keep talking. And next time (if there IS a next time), you can bet she'll pay attention in class when the teacher discusses the *Arabian Nights...*

BY SARAH ALBEE

SARAH ZODD'S ARABIAN NIGHTS

"My doze itches," said Owen, shifting uncomfortably. His red nose twitched. His heavy chains clanked.

"That's the least of our worries right now," I said, looking around the damp cell. "Considering we're probably going to be boiled in oil and then chopped into little pieces in the morning."

"Yeeeeeesh," we both said. It's safe to say that I, Sarah Zodd, and he, Owen Philips, were two unhappy kids.

Both of us were slumped on the dirty stone floor. Our hands were above our heads, manacled to the wall. One of each of our feet was chained in a heavy iron bracelet attached to a big, round, metal ball that weighed about two tons.

"And HE doesn't make me feel much better," I muttered, gesturing with my chin toward the tiny barred opening on the door. Sure enough, as it had been doing every few minutes, an enormous face appeared at the window and leered

at us, revealing large, snaggly teeth. The guard held up what appeared to be his favorite metal instrument of torture, and clanked it against the bars. Then he gave a low, evil laugh.

I closed my eyes and shook my head, which was pounding. Just yesterday, we had been sitting next to each other in Mr. Eames's class. How had we gotten into this mess?

TO BE CONTINUED

LUNCH BOX **DAY 1** LIBRARY

LUNCH NOTES:

_____

_____

_____

_____

_____

_____

_____

SARAH ZODD'S ARABIAN NIGHTS

THE STORY SO FAR...

Sarah and Owen are chained to a wall in a dismal dungeon. Owen's cold is growing worse by the minute.

Owen and I are best friends. Sometimes people are surprised to hear this. I'm quiet and he's loud. I never talk in class. He never STOPS talking. But somehow we get along great.

Our regular fifth-grade teacher is Ms. Gibbs. She is the best teacher ever. But one Monday the principal told us Ms. Gibbs had to have her appendix taken out. So we were going to get a substitute teacher for a few weeks. His name was Mr. Eames, but everyone soon started calling him Mean Eames.

He never smiled. And he gave us weird homework projects. For instance, this week we each had to read a story from the *Arabian Nights,* then do an oral report on it for the class. That meant standing up in front of the class and

talking, something I hated to do.

Yesterday, a Friday, had begun badly. First, Owen was catching a cold. Whenever he gets a cold, he loses his voice. So he was pretty grumpy. Then Mean Eames called on me to do my report about "The Fisherman and the Genie." While Mean Eames was still talking, Owen slipped me a piece of paper. He'd drawn a pretty funny picture and written "Mean Eames" below it.

I giggled. Then I became aware of someone standing behind me. Slowly I swiveled my head . . . straight up into the scowling face of Mean Eames.

TO BE CONTINUED

LUNCH BOX **DAY** ·2· LIBRARY

LUNCH NOTES:

_____

_____

_____

_____

_____

_____

_____

THE STORY SO FAR...

Sarah remembered that yesterday Mean Eames caught her laughing at Owen's funny picture of him.

Of course, Mean Eames assumed I had drawn it. He didn't yell. He just said, "Sarah, you can do an EXTRA *Arabian Nights* report for Monday. Now let's hear today's assignment."

I stammered out my "Fisherman and the Genie" report. Then I stumbled back to my desk and tried to make myself disappear. It didn't work, of course.

MEAN EAMES

The next day was Saturday. I called Owen and invited him to a yard sale around the corner.

"I thig I'b geddig a cold," he protested. His voice sounded awful. But I talked him into coming.

Tables had been set up all over the lawn. We sorted through some junk. Owen picked up an old, beat-up metal thing. It looked like a longish teapot. "Straighd out of the Arabiad Dights!" he said grinning. "Maybe idz MAGIC!" I didn't pay much attention to him. And who could understand the guy with that cold?

Suddenly, Owen gripped my arm. "Loog over there!" he croaked. It was Mean Eames.

"I *do not* want to see him!" I whispered to Owen. I turned and tried to push him toward the side of the house so we could creep out. I guess my tee shirt must have brushed up against the lamp in his hand. The next thing I knew the yard had disappeared in a cloud of blue smoke.

TO BE CONTINUED

LUNCH NOTES:

_____

_____

_____

_____

_____

_____

_____

THE STORY SO FAR...

Sarah remembered that at the yard sale she accidentally rubbed the lamp; everything disappeared in a cloud of smoke.

SARAH ZODD'S ARABIAN NIGHTS

DAY · 4 ·

When the smoke cleared, we found ourselves face down on a pile of rocks. At least, they felt like rocks. We scrambled to our hands and knees and looked at each other.

"I guess that *was* a magic lamp," I said. "And this looks like a cave full of priceless jewels." Owen nodded, speechless.

Owen recovered his voice, or what was left of it. "Loog ad thad!" he bleated. He had picked up something in the piles of rubies and diamonds. It was a huge blue stone that had some shimmery white lines in it. "A rare forb of the bineral corundub! Otherwise node as a star sapphire!"

He was still babbling when I felt a large hand clap me on the shoulder. I was pulled roughly to my feet. A large,

heavily armed man stood before me. Even if he hadn't been missing several teeth, I still wouldn't have liked his smile. A moment later, he grabbed Owen, too.

"Stealing the Sultan's jewels, are you?" he said to Owen in a low, cruel voice.

As usual, Owen tried to talk his way out of it. "Oh, doh, sir. I was simbly examinig this egsquisid egsample of a . . ."

"Silence!" the man thundered. Then he turned toward the dozen or so soldiers standing behind him. "Take this boy thief and the girl to the dungeon," he told them. Then he turned to face us again. "See you in about 80 years," he said, laughing unpleasantly. "If you're lucky."

TO BE CONTINUED

LUNCH NOTES:

SARAH ZODD'S ARABIAN NIGHTS

THE STORY SO FAR...

Owen and Sarah were caught with the Sultan's jewels and thrown in a dungeon.

And that's how we found ourselves chained up in a dungeon. They seemed to think Owen was the thief. I was just some dumb tag-along. But we were both in the soup.

Suddenly, the head guard's face loomed in the window again. "The Sultan wants to see you," he growled. With a loud jingling of keys, he entered the cell and unlocked our chains. "Let's go," said the guard. We went.

We climbed about a hundred flights of stone stairs, and then suddenly we were squinting in a blaze of flickering lamps. It wasn't hard to pick out which guy was the Sultan: he reclined on a jeweled couch, eating grapes from a golden bowl. He wore a sparkly robe and had an unpleasant little pointy beard. "Come forward!" he commanded. We did.

"Who sent you to steal my treasure? Speak, boy!"

Owen tried, but by now his voice was only a whisper.

"You refuse to speak? Since you mock me, I order you to die a cruel death at sunrise tomorrow! Guards! Take him away!"

Things were not looking good for Owen. I'm not used to talking my way out of scrapes, but it took just one glance at the sneering Sultan, and another glance at the guard, who grinned and plinked his ugly-looking blade, and I hatched a plan.

TO BE CONTINUED

LUNCH BOX **DAY · 5 ·** LIBRARY

LUNCH NOTES:

_____

_____

_____

_____

_____

_____

_____

SARAH ZODD'S ARABIAN NIGHTS

THE STORY SO FAR...

The Sultan condemned Owen to death, but Sarah hatches a plan to save him.

"Wait! Wait!" I squeaked. The guards paused. The Sultan looked surprised. "Do you think that it would be OK if I told my friend one last story before he's taken away? It being his last night on Earth and all? He just loves a good story." Owen started to say something, but my quick jab in the ribs shut him right up.

The Sultan shrugged, but he looked interested. "Proceed."

I felt a tiny bit grateful toward Mr. Eames. See, the whole idea of the *Arabian Nights* is that a mean king condemns a maiden to die in the morning. So she tells him a story that is so exciting that she gets to live an extra day in order to finish the tale. But she never really finishes it. She keeps stringing the mean king along with exciting stories until he forgets why he wanted to kill her in the first place. All I had to do, I figured, was mesmerize the Sultan with an exciting story, just as the maiden had done, and then leave him hanging. At least it might buy us time, so we could escape. I tried to recall how my "Fisherman and the Genie" story was supposed to go. Talk about pressure. Trying not to be nervous in class was nothing compared with trying to keep my best friend from being chopped into little bits.

"OK," I began. "So there was once this, uh, fisherman. He was, uh, fishing. No. Wait." I had to start over. This plan wasn't working very well. "Once, there was this fisherman."

"SILENCE!" shouted the Sultan. "You have bored us long enough! Kill them BOTH in the morning!"

TO BE CONTINUED

LUNCH NOTES:

_____

_____

_____

_____

_____

_____

_____

THE STORY SO FAR...

Sarah's plan failed. Now they're both going to die in the morning.

SARAH ZODD'S ARABIAN NIGHTS

DAY · 7 ·

"No, hold on!" My words tumbled out. "This fisherman was really clever and handsome. Sort of like you, Your Highness!" The Sultan lifted a bejeweled index finger, and the guards retreated.

"So one day, he cast his net and pulled in an old bottle. He uncorked it, and out swirled a huge genie. 'Prepare to die!' it said."

"'But why?' cried the fisherman. 'I have just rescued you!'"

"'For the first ten thousand years of my captivity,' said the genie, 'I vowed to bestow vast riches on whomever rescued me—camels, jewels, all you can eat at McDonald's . . . '"

"Who is this King McDonald?" interrupted the Sultan.

"Uh, it's far away from here," I said, and continued hastily. "'And for the next ten thousand years,' said the genie, 'I vowed to bestow MORE riches on whomever rescued me—castles, gold, a gift certificate at the Gap . . . '"

"The what?" asked the guard, who had edged closer to listen.

"Oh. Ah. It's a, uh, great marketplace," I said lamely, and pushed on. "'But then I got so angry that no one had rescued me for 20,000 years, I vowed to kill whoever finally did, since they hadn't come along sooner. So prepare yourself to die!'"

I yawned loudly. "Good night, Your Highness."

"Hey!" cried the Sultan. "What happened next?"

"Would you like me to continue the story tomorrow?"

"Very well," said the Sultan. "I will spare your lives for one day. But just to find out how the story ends!"

TO BE CONTINUED

LUNCH BOX **DAY · 7 ·** LIBRARY

LUNCH NOTES:

_____

_____

_____

_____

_____

_____

_____

THE STORY SO FAR...

The Sultan spared the lives of Sarah and Owen for one more day so he can find out how the story ends.

SARAH ZODD'S ARABIAN NIGHTS

The next night

Owen and I were brought back before the Sultan. Owen's voice was still only a whisper. I was going to have to do all the talking. The Sultan, who seemed in a better mood, had permitted us to sit down on a thick rug near his feet. I noticed that the guards had stationed themselves closer than they had been the night before, even though they were pretending not to listen.

"The fisherman bowed before the genie," I began. "Then he said, 'Oh, great genie! You are truly all-powerful and all-knowing. I will prepare myself to die. But first, I just wanted to mention that I happened to look inside your bottle and couldn't help but notice that you've left your iron on.'"

"What is an Ironon?" demanded the Sultan.

"It's a, um, magical tool," I replied. "So the genie swooped back inside his bottle to turn it off, and the fisherman quickly stopped it back up with the cork. Then he chucked the bottle into the ocean."

The Sultan stared at me for a moment. The whole room was silent. Slowly he began to laugh. All the guards joined in. Owen and I weren't sure what to do, so we started to laugh, too. Owen sounded like a diseased goose.

"That was a good story," said the Sultan, wiping a mirthful tear from the corner of his eye. "Too bad you have to die tomorrow morning."

TO BE CONTINUED

LUNCH BOX **DAY 8** LIBRARY

LUNCH NOTES:

_____

_____

_____

_____

_____

_____

_____

THE STORY SO FAR...

The Sultan liked Sarah's story, but still intends to execute them both the next day.

SARAH ZODD'S ARABIAN NIGHTS

I kicked myself for having ended the story. "Did I mention," I cried desperately, "that the fisherman had a cousin?"

"No," said the Sultan. "What about him?"

"Well. The cousin was a sailor. He went on a voyage with a huge ship laden with treasures."

"Gold, jewels, and Ironons?" asked the Sultan eagerly.

"Precisely," I replied. "He and his comrades sailed around for a few weeks, until one day they were blown off course. 'Rock ho!' cried the lookout. They'd barely had time to put on their goggles and waterwings before they crashed into the rock and were swept into the sea. They all managed to swim to shore. But then the ground started to shake. And guess what came stomping over the hill?"

"WHAT?" shouted the head guard.

"A huge, ugly, drooling, one-eyed giant," I replied.

"NO!" said the Sultan breathlessly. "What happened?"

"The giant gathered up all the sailors in his big hairy arms and brought them to his cave. He picked up the captain of the ship and carried him into the kitchen. Then . . . Why, would you LOOK at the time!" I interrupted myself brightly. "Shall I go on with the story tomorrow night?"

The Sultan frowned. "Very well. I COMMAND you to continue tomorrow." Owen and I had been spared another day.

TO BE CONTINUED

LUNCH NOTES:

SARAH ZODD'S ARABIAN NIGHTS

THE STORY SO FAR...

This time Sarah stopped in the middle of the story. She and Owen were spared for another day.

My plan was working. During the day, Owen and I would work on the evening's story, trying to get it as exciting as possible. His voice was returning, but we both agreed I should keep doing the talking. To secure Owen's position, I'd explained to the Sultan how Owen helped me to think up the stories I told.

The next night we discovered that the Sultan had ordered couches for both of us to lie on. Reclining on my couch, I continued my story.

"As the captain was saying his prayers, the giant sat down at the table and ate a huge meal. It looked like roast antelope or something, and it was pretty greasy and disgusting. He spit the bones out all over the floor. Then the giant stood up and turned to the captain. He tossed him an enormous sponge, and, with grunts and gestures, told the captain to clean the kitchen."

"Yecccch," said the Sultan and the head guard together.

"Yes," I agreed. "It was a nasty job. And this went on night after night. The giant would eat his dinner, and then select one of the prisoners to clean up the kitchen. They were miserable. So they decided to escape."

"How did they do that?" The Sultan had sprung up from his couch. Then he saw me yawn, and sat down meekly. "Tomorrow night?" he asked.

With a wink at Owen, I nodded. "Tomorrow night."

TO BE CONTINUED

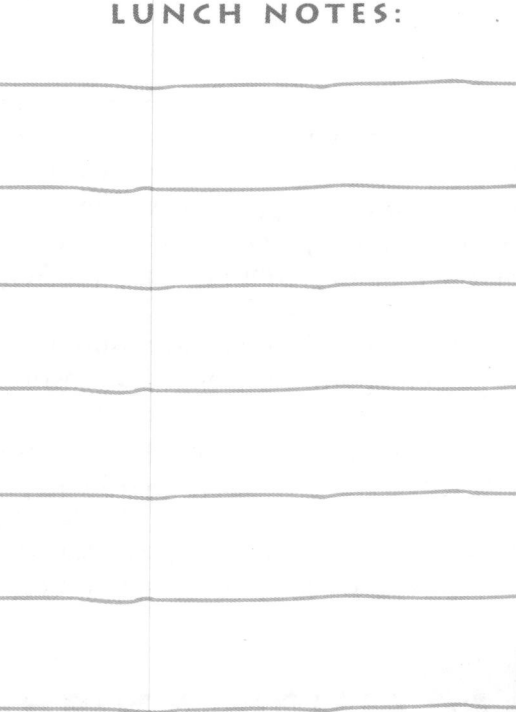

LUNCH BOX **DAY 10** LIBRARY

LUNCH NOTES:

SARAH ZODD'S ARABIAN NIGHTS

THE STORY SO FAR...

Sarah was about to tell the Sultan how the giant's prisoners planned to escape.

"Let's see, where was I?" I said the next night. Owen and I were dressed in costly robes. A slave fanned us and peeled us grapes as I talked.

"Oh, yes. The prisoners had built a getaway raft out of the giant's discarded ice-pop sticks. That night, when the giant's back was turned, they all put on their swimming goggles. Then the sailor picked up a huge paring knife, and hacked at a huge onion. The giant roared and put his hands to his one eye, which began gushing tears. As the blinded giant thrashed, the men ran out the door, hopped onto the raft, and escaped.

"They were all rescued by a passing ship. But our sailor was swept away by an enormous wave. He managed to cling to some driftwood and washed up on another strange island. The natives took him to meet their king. The sailor immediately became a favorite at the court, because he taught the king's Royal Chef how to make pizza."

"Pizza?" asked the Sultan. "What is that?"

"A meal for kings, Sir," I replied. "The king loved pizza so much, he gave the sailor a little white poodle to thank him. But very soon, the poor sailor would make a terrible discovery about life on this island."

We rose. The Sultan drooped. Popping a last grape into my mouth, I saluted him good night.

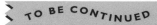
TO BE CONTINUED

LUNCH BOX DAY · 11 · LIBRARY

LUNCH NOTES:

_____

_____

_____

_____

_____

_____

_____

THE STORY SO FAR...

The sailor in Sarah's story was on the brink of making a terrible discovery about life on the island.

SARAH ZODD'S ARABIAN NIGHTS

DAY · 12 ·

"So?" said the Sultan eagerly. It was the next night. Owen and I were having a late supper. We had taught the Royal Chef how to make pizza, and he had done a respectable job.

"The sailor lived happily in this kingdom for some time," I said. "He became pretty chummy with his next-door neighbor. So when the neighbor's pet canary died, the sailor went over to console him. He found his neighbor weeping uncontrollably. 'There, there,' said the sailor. 'You'll get another pet bird soon.' The neighbor looked at him and said, 'Don't you know? In this country, when a pet dies, its owner has to be buried along with his pet!'

"The sailor's eyes widened in horror. He ran home to check on his poodle's health, and was just in time to see it breathe its last

gasp, having consumed both of the sailor's bedroom slippers."

"So the sailor had to be buried along with his dog?" the Sultan asked. "But how unfair!"

"Wasn't it?" I agreed. "Dog and sailor were laid out on a splendid doggie bed, and lowered into a big tomb. A heavy rock was moved in place, and all was darkness and silence." I stood up. "See you tomorrow," I said, and Owen and I walked upstairs to our lavish chambers.

As we climbed, Owen elbowed me and hissed, "Did you see the lamp? It was sitting right there on the Sultan's table!"

TO BE CONTINUED

LUNCH NOTES:

THE STORY SO FAR...

Owen spotted the magic lamp on the Sultan's table. Now he's the one with a plan.

SARAH ZODD'S ARABIAN NIGHTS

The next night I finished up my tale. "Down in the tomb, the sailor heard a tiny rustle. It was a mouse. It scampered off toward a tiny dim light in the distance. He followed the mouse, and emerged in blinding sunlight, on a beach. On the horizon he spied a sail. He waved wildly, and the ship saw him and rescued him."

"Good story!" clapped the Sultan. "Tell me another!"

I looked meaningfully at Owen. It was time to act. "Your Highness?" I said. "As your trusted advisors, Owen and I have had an idea. It involves your personal happiness. We think that it is time you found yourself a wife."

"A wife?" echoed the Sultan. He looked intrigued.

"Yessir. And we thought that perhaps we could help you find one. We thought you might invite all the interested maidens in the kingdom to come here and audition for our position as royal storyteller. Whoever tells the best stories gets the job, as well as your hand in marriage."

The Sultan mulled it over. After a moment or two he beamed. "Great idea!" he cried. "I insist on giving you a thank-you present!"

The plan had worked. "Hmmm," I said, pretending to think.

"How about a poodle?"

"No thanks," Owen shuddered.

As casually as I could, I looked around the room. "That sure is a nice lamp," I said. "How about that?"

The Sultan sprang to his feet. "GUARDS!" he roared.

TO BE CONTINUED

LUNCH BOX DAY 13 LIBRARY

LUNCH NOTES:

THE STORY SO FAR...

The Sultan liked Sarah and Owen's plan, but seemed angered when Sarah asked for the lamp as a gift.

SARAH ZODD'S ARABIAN NIGHTS · DAY 14 ·

Owen and I looked at each other in alarm. The Sultan was pointing at the lamp. "GUARDS!" he yelled again. With a stampede of footsteps and a clattering of metal, a few dozen guards hustled in and stood at attention before the Sultan. He handed one of them the lamp. "Take this to gift wrapping!" he demanded. "And then call forth all the maidens in the kingdom who have an interest in both marriage and public speaking!" The guards hustled out.

The Sultan turned to Owen and me and smiled. He looked downright pleasant. "We'll have the auditions tomorrow afternoon."

I had to hand it to Owen. He'd convinced me that the Sultan would go for the wife idea.

I suppose once we had the lamp, Owen and I could have ducked out immediately. But we were curious to see what kind of turnout there would be for our replacement. So the next afternoon, refreshed from having been bathed and oiled at the Royal Baths, Owen and I came to the auditions. The head guard had been promoted to royal casting director. He stood at the doorway importantly calling out names. The courtyard was full of beautiful maidens. A few of them paced up and down, quietly reciting lines. The guard bellowed "NEXT!" That was the last thing we heard as we rubbed the lamp.

TO BE CONTINUED

LUNCH BOX **DAY · 14 ·** LIBRARY

LUNCH NOTES:

_____

_____

_____

_____

_____

_____

_____

SARAH ZODD'S ARABIAN NIGHTS · DAY 15 ·

THE STORY SO FAR...

The Sultan gave Sarah and Owen the magic lamp. They stayed a bit longer to see their plan enacted, then rubbed the lamp.

With a puff of blue smoke, we found ourselves back at the sale, just where we'd been standing when we left. Owen was still holding the lamp. No one seemed to have noticed anything. "Look," said Owen, pointing at the lamp.

It had a large crack in it, all the way from top to bottom. "It probably doesn't work anymore," I said. "Although I'm not about to rub it again to find out."

Owen nodded. Then he sniffed on purpose. "My cold is gone, so it must have really happened."

"Hello, Sarah. Hello, Owen," said a voice. It was Mean Eames. But he looked, well, nice.

"Hey, Mr. Eames." I said, and shook his hand. "I'm really sorry about how I behaved in your class yesterday."

"That's OK, Sarah," he replied, and smiled. Then he looked at the lamp in Owen's hand. "What a terrific lamp, Owen. It looks like it's straight out of an *Arabian Nights* story!" And he laughed heartily. Owen and I did too, but ours was a hollow laugh. "Are you planning to buy that?" he asked. Owen and I shook our heads violently. "Then maybe I will!" said Mr. Eames.

Well, what would YOU have done in our shoes? Mr. Eames would never believe us if we told him the truth. Besides, he'd be a good match for the Sultan.

So we handed him the lamp. Then Owen and I walked quickly away.

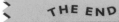

THE END

LUNCH BOX DAY 15 LIBRARY

LUNCH NOTES: